Inside
and
other short fiction

Inside

and
other short fiction

Japanese women
by Japanese women

WITH A FOREWORD BY
Ruth Ozeki

compiled by Cathy Layne

KODANSHA INTERNATIONAL
Tokyo • New York • London

The stories in this collection were originally published in Japanese, and were selected from the following publications: "Milk" (*Miruku*, 2004) from *Miruku* (Chuokoron Shinsha, Tokyo 2004); "Inside" (*Inside*, 2004) from *Teenage* (Futabasha, Tokyo 2004); "Piss" (*Pisu*, 1997) from *Pisu* (Kodansha Bunko, 2002); "My Son's Lips" (*Musuko no kuchibiru*, 2000) from *Musuko no kuchibiru* (Kadokawa Bunko, 2003); "Her Room" (*Kanojo no heya*, 2003) from *Kanojo no heya* (Kodansha, Tokyo 2003); "Fiesta" (*Fiesuta*, 2001) from *Himegimi* (Bungei Shunju, Tokyo 2001); "The Unfertilized Egg" (*Museiran*, 2004) from *Hatsuga* (Magazine House, Tokyo 2004); "The Shadow of the Orchid" (*Ran no kage*, 1998) from *Ran no kage* (Shincho Bunko, Tokyo 2000)

Distributed in the United States by Kodansha America, Inc., and in the United Kingdom and continental Europe by Kodansha Europe Ltd.

Published by Kodansha International Ltd., 17–14 Otawa 1-chome, Bunkyo-ku, Tokyo 112–8625, and Kodansha America, Inc.

First edition, 2006
15 14 13 12 11 10 09 08 07 06   10 9 8 7 6 5 4 3 2 1

Library of Congress Catalog-in-Publication Data available

www.kodansha-intl.com

CONTENTS

FOREWORD

When I was a little half-Japanese girl growing up in rural New England, the old guy who worked at the feed store used to pinch my cheeks and call me "Suzy." I thought this was very special, to have my own nickname, so much so that for many years, whenever I got a new doll, I named her "Suzy," too. The old guy had fought in the Pacific during World War II, and I didn't realize until much later that he had named me, a six-year-old half-Japanese girl, after the Chinese prostitute Suzy Wong, of the eponymous film.

Recently I saw an ad for a California-based skateboard company, which featured a different vision of Japanese womanhood: an *anime*-style image of a saucer-eyed, knock-kneed schoolgirl, dressed in a blood-splattered, miniskirted school uniform and sailor blouse, carrying a chain saw and dragging a severed head.

Hmm.

The popular perception of Japanese women has certainly undergone a transformation in the past century. No longer the docile, submissive Madame Butterfly of the early 1900s, or the docile, submissive pan-pan or geesha-girl of the post-World War II occupation, or the docile, submissive office lady or salaryman's wife of the 1980s and '90s, the image of women in modern Japan now seems poised to evolve into something altogether new. In recent years, the popular imagination has begun to depict women with a new kind of agency and autonomy. The new Japanese woman is not only redefining her sexual prowess; she is even acquiring supernatural powers: the demure schoolgirl has morphed into a superheroine, or antiheroine, out to save or to destroy the world.

But do these images (still so often derived from the male imagination and drawn by his hand) correspond with the reality of Japanese women today? Japanese society is undergoing radical change. The traditional family, whose ballast was the stay-at-home wife and mother, is breaking down. Marriage and birth rates are declining, while the divorce rate is escalating. Career opportunities for women, too, are on the rise, and many women opt to marry later, or not at all. As a result of these and other social factors, Japanese women today have more economic and sexual freedom than ever before. In what ways are women adapting to the radically different Japan of the new millennium? Have their self-images changed, and how?

Being a writer and a reader, I look to literature to provide the answers to these questions. Luckily, the female literary imagination is evidenced earlier in Japan than in any other country or culture in the world; its initial flowering, at the beginning of the last millennium, culminated in what is often cited as the world's first novel, *The Tale of Genji*, by Lady Murasaki Shikibu. A best-seller in the Heian Court a thousand years ago, it is a story that centers around the exploits of a single male romantic hero, but its strength lies in its female characters, Genji's many lovers. Reading it, one can't help but think that Genji himself serves largely as a foil to deliver up this remarkable diversity of Heian womanhood, and that indeed the women are the focus of the author's primary interest and attention. And contemporary with Lady Murasaki is another favorite woman writer of mine, Sei Shonagon, the author of the famous *Pillow Book*, a humorous and poetic commentary on Heian Court mores and manners, which includes a running and often acerbic critique of Sei's own many bumbling male lovers.

Now fast forward a thousand years or so. Japanese women are still prolific writers today. These contemporary authors often focus on relationships and sexuality, themes explored by their female ancestors one thousand years ago. But sadly, although many of us in the West have heard of Lady Murasaki and Sei Shonagon, few have heard of Tamaki Daido, or Yuzuki Muroi, or Nobuko Takagi. Their work has not been available in English translation.

The eight stories that make up this anthology, *Inside and other short fiction: Japanese women by Japanese women*, address this dearth. Most of the authors contained herein are prizewinning popular Japanese novelists who have never before been published in English, and their stories paint a picture of contemporary Japanese women's lives that is fresh, new, and possibly even shocking to readers in the West.

The stories reflect the experiences of a wide diversity of Japanese women. Three of the stories are told by teens. In "Milk," a teenage girl leads us into her world, where adult men date middle-school girls, where friendships and fashions drift and waver, and sex is as fickle as the changing weather. In the title story, "Inside," another very different teenager struggles with her ambivalence toward her boyfriend's wish for intimacy as she watches her parents' marriage dissolve. "Piss" tells the sexually explicit story of a gutsy and yet strangely innocent nineteen-year-old prostitute who, on her twentieth birthday, in the aftermath of cruel abuse and betrayal, finds the courage to go on.

Working women are the heroines of three of the stories. In "My Son's Lips," a working mother finds her multiple roles tipped into confusion after an accidental meeting with a cabdriver and his wife. The thirty-six-year-old single narrator of "The Unfertilized Egg" mulls over her deteriorating affair with her married boss, while eating bowls of tapioca pudding and dreaming about eggs. And in the comical allegory "Fiesta," a sexually repressed office lady's cantankerous Desire forms an alliance with her Murderous Intent to triumph over her other emotions, including her Obsession, Passion, Reason, and Pride.

"Her Room" is the subtle, disturbing tale of a divorced woman, cursed with niceness, who is pursued by a painfully awkward and annoying misfit who wants to be her friend. And finally, "The Shadow of the Orchid" is the wonderfully compelling story of a fifty-year-old woman, the wife of a doctor, who is haunted by a gaudy orchid that belonged to a beautiful young cancer patient who died in her husband's care.

The stories are, by turns, delicate and explicit, haunting and aggressive, tender and titillating, poignant and comical. They tackle everything from emerging sexuality, to love, abuse, perversion, motherhood, divorce, and finally death. And while diverse in their tone and content, what these eight stories share is a fearless and unsentimental narrative gaze that is fixed unblinkingly on the female experience in Japan today.

Japanese women have indeed come a long way from the world of geesha-girls and Madame Butterfly. How far? Turn the page and see.

Ruth Ozeki

Milk

Tamaki Daido

He didn't choose Akina, even though she's the cutest of the four of us. But nobody made a big deal out of it. I guess you'd call Akina beautiful rather than cute. When we take pictures in a photo booth, she always looks as if she's sitting further from the camera, her face is so tiny and delicate. Her grandfather or someone was supposed to have been Russian. She's so perfect she doesn't look human—it's amazing. That's why guys are always too shy to talk to her. Usually guys go for about the third hottest one in a group. It's the easy and safe choice. Until now, that had been my role.

"So you're going? You're gonna go out with him?" Namiko, our number two, won't quit teasing Masumi.

And, of course, Masumi totally overreacts: "No way! No way! I can't—I just can't," she says, shaking her head wildly. She's turned beet red. Being fourth in the group, this is her first time to get a guy. (And an older guy too!) She must be freaking out. "Akina-chan!" She grabs hold of Akina's hand like she's begging for help. Masumi has two older sisters, so playing the baby is her forte. She looks like she's going to cry, but she is sooo faking it. Akina just coolly watches the exchange between Namiko and Masumi. She doesn't say a word. I'm walking right behind Akina and can see how totally unfazed she is.

The wind's really cold. It's the season for eating simmered *oden* in hot soup, and steaming, fluffy meat dumplings. The four of us look like a bunch of retards, we're so identically dressed. We're all wearing the cardigans that are totally in among the girls at our school. We bugged our parents until they bought us one. To tell the truth, they cost under ten thousand yen—if you found a job at some sleazy place in the city, you could probably earn that much in a night—but these are something you have to wear at school, or around parents and neighbors, so you can't buy them secretly. And they have to look at least a little bit square. They're off-white, with a leaf logo on the chest. Men's L size, pretty comfortable to wear. You leave them buttoned and pull them on over your head, and it feels like you're wrapping up your whole body in them. "They look sloppy, and if you're going to have to roll them up to make them fit, then buy one that fits properly in the first place—in a dark color like navy blue or gray," was what the teachers said. No matter how much the student council tried to fight it, it was useless. Looks like they're going to be banned. No problem, we'll just give up and start something new. In middle school, eighth graders basically rule. Maybe we'll make navy blue or gray neatly fitting cardigans the next fad.

"Go on, go out with him! You'll be totally famous at school. You know—scoring an outsider." This is Namiko's advice to Masumi.

"Outsider?" Akina bursts out laughing.

"I can't!" Masumi's face just won't go back to its usual shade. Maybe she really doesn't like him that much. Could be she really isn't into love and that kind of thing yet. Well, her family is seriously into breeding budgerigars. Right from the moment you go in the front door the whole place is, like, packed with birdcages.

Namiko won't give up. She's picking on Masumi way too much, which makes it totally obvious she's pissed off that the architect guy (he does drawings, or something, in some kind of designer's office) didn't pick her. On this street, there's a tobacconist's, a convenience store, and a bunch of other tiny two-story buildings all jumbled together. We just passed the little building where the architect guy has his office. Every day, about the time we go by on our way home from school, he'll be pretending to be taking a cigarette break, leaning on the fire escape, wrapped up in an oversized coat that makes him look like some kind of magician. But he isn't there today. Yesterday he handed a letter to Masumi. He must be pretty nervous today, wondering whether she's read it or not.

To tell the truth, we're starting to feel a bit uncomfortable. It's kind of retarded really—adult men going out with middle-school girls. Up to now we'd been kind of joshing him and stuff, but looking at his face when he handed the letter to Masumi, we felt a bit sorry for him. When I say *joshing*, it was like we'd all yell out, "Don't work too hard!" and then he'd shout something back, and that was cool. That was enough really . . .

The letter asks Masumi to go to the festival at a nearby college. By *college*, he actually means the night school. So the festival's at night

Milk

too. That is sooo lame. Everyone's so busy with working and studying that they're completely wiped. Do people really date at that kind of festival? But I guess it might be okay having it at night . . . Lazy catch-a-goldfish, a tired bazaar, weary mini-concert—something to josh the guy about a bit more. From now on, the rest of us can hang back and watch how love develops between Masumi and the architect guy. At least it looks like that's how it's going to be.

After we first noticed the guy, we used to hang around and shriek if we saw him, waving and jumping up and down, and shriek again if he waved back. Well, it worked—it got him interested anyway. (If you did that with a guy at school, or an "insider" if you like, he wouldn't go for it. He'd get mad and accuse you of picking on him. I guess that would be the normal response.) But then, after the same thing for two months, I guess the guy got fed up with it. At which point he was pretty smart. He chose the one of us that really stood out. Oh yeah, he made an awesome choice: Masumi of the frizzy hair and bug eyes. I just don't get adult tastes. All this time he was being friendly to us because of Masumi?

Akina's right hand is in Masumi's and her left in Namiko's. She's smiling to herself as she watches the two of them. Underneath that expression for sure she's thinking, boooring . . . Not that she hates her friends—she's just bored. We're soul mates, Akina and I. All four of us get on well, but Akina and I, we mesh. Well, we haven't actually tested whether we really do mesh. It wouldn't be right to just go off together, and anyway if we did, the group would break up. I guess being soul mates doesn't really mean that much anyway.

I haven't really got any problems at home. I guess I'm lucky. All I've got to worry about is whether or not to go out with Ryuji Toshima. That's because I'm happy and have no pressures. I took entrance exams for a high school that was about my level. It was a breeze, and my parents are going to pay for it too, so I've nothing to complain about. So, as I need something to worry about, I've decided Ryuji Toshima's going to be it. Love will do for a start. And it's something I can talk about with friends. Well, you don't talk about serious problems, right? You don't burden your best friends with the really heavy stuff.

To tell the truth, I was really into a guy on the baseball team, two years above us. But he graduated and went to one of those high schools with a good baseball team. If someone suddenly disappears from your life like that, love naturally dies. But my heart still aches whenever I think of him. When I was on a family trip to Shikoku and saw someone who looked like this guy, I nearly cried with happiness. Even though it couldn't have been him, it seemed as though fate had brought us together again. To yearn for the love of the same person for your whole life, it's like a woman from the olden days. It's classic. It has a kind of snap to it, like when you bite into a hot dog sausage. Hey, cool—it turns out I might actually know what love feels like. I think I'll keep the whole thing secret. For about ten years. The love of my life—him alone. *No matter how much my body may be soiled, until the day I can offer it to this man, I will always be a virgin in my heart.* No, not quite right . . . *In my dreams I have been in his arms many times.* That's it. Yeah, that sounds pretty cool.

But it looks like Akina does have them, serious troubles. When I say *serious*, I don't really know how bad. Complicated family problems, maybe. She's like the heroine in a story, Akina. Wherever she goes, whatever she does, it's dramatic. Mind you, I might be reading meaning into things, like I was watching some soap opera. And truthfully, I've never seen a seriously dramatic scene yet. It just feels like I'm going to sometime. I can't wait. The real Akina never makes a big deal out of things. She stays in the background, puts her own problems to one side, and takes care of her friends. Sometimes you think, "Hey, did she look a bit sad just now?" but she quickly hides it under a poker face.

Can you come to our college festival on November 15 at 6 p.m.? I finish work at five and then I'm going there with a friend. Do you get out of school around five? If you can make it by six, that'd be great. Let's try to win a goldfish or something.

Namiko has got hold of the letter and is reading it over and over. "You call this asking someone out? This is so creepy."

Looks like he thought it would appeal to a middle-school student if he wrote it on pastel blue paper. With a picture of a kitten. He's got quite nice handwriting. Masumi's expression is so funny. How long can she keep up a face like that? She'd better quit it, otherwise Namiko is going to give her an even harder time. My mom once said that she thinks Masumi is the cutest one of us. That in the future she's going to be the happiest. When I was like, "Huh? But she's such a nerd," she's like, "Yes, but that's only temporary. Masumi-chan will grow up fast. You'll understand one day—when you're grown up. Men notice that kind of girl first. She's going to be really popular, you'll see." And when I'm like, "But what about Akina? She's always number one," again she's like, "Yes, but only for now." And that's all she'll say. In the group, we don't really care that much about Masumi, so I didn't pay much attention to what my mom said. It's scary how little reality there is behind my mom's theories. Like she conjures them up out of nowhere. It's dangerous to let yourself be persuaded by what she says. She doesn't care if things are true or not, she just talks about what's sure to happen—that's my mom.

"Whoa, this is such a big deal for you. Go for it then. We'll be here for you." Namiko still won't back off. Finally, her attention turns to me. "Komugi, how much money have you got? Can you lend me some?"

I'm like, "Sure, I'll buy." But really I hate the whole subject of money. I feel depressed if I lend someone ten yen. But I can't refuse. I just try to forget as quickly as possible that I ever lent it.

Even after we've been into the convenience store to buy *oden* and are squatting down near the trash cans at the front to eat it, the conversation is still about the architect guy. Akina is sitting by herself on the guardrail. The three of us chose to squat next to the trash cans while Akina chose to park her butt on the guardrail. Our lives are mapped out by the trivial choices we make. Seriously. I steal glances at Akina's face as she skillfully picks up a whole beef-tendon kebab with her chopsticks and crams it into her mouth. Then there's Namiko who has accidentally mashed her hard-boiled egg into her soup and is now having to slurp it down; Masumi who can't quite get a grip on her jellylike *konnyaku* yam with her chopsticks; and me fighting a losing battle with a mouth stuffed full of *konnyaku* noodles. I was already regretting not getting something easier to swallow.

I think we need one more person in the group. Akina is unshakably in the number one spot. Seeing as fourth-out-of-four Masumi has got herself a real guy, it's dumb, but I guess we have to give her credit. It really raises her status. A number five friend, organized and quiet, and from a one-parent family. That would work. That's the same as Akina, except fifth. I'd like to see a girl like that. Less hot even than Masumi. Me and Namiko and Masumi, we're all disorganized and quiet and still have both parents. There's not much to choose between the three of us. We take it in turns to be second, third, and fourth. Our looks, our personalities, our grades at school are all pretty much the same. So it's clear we need a number five. Leading an unhappy life but totally able to appreciate the little things. Someone who can be satisfied with being that—an obviously bottom-of-the-pile number five . . . But come to think of it, it is the spring term of eighth grade. Everyone's about to graduate. I guess there's no point in making new friends at this place.

When I moved up to middle school from elementary, I was a bit surprised at how unfriendly the place was. Unwanted crap was cut off and thrown away. The dumb kids had always been in class with us and just sort of pushed through, but in middle school the teachers started to dump them, letting them hide out at the nurse's office.

People who were itching to rebel were marked and watched. But no moves were made. They were just watched. When they finally did rebel, they were caught. Then there were those of us who kind of slid by trying not to catch the teachers' eye. Well, the teachers couldn't be bothered with us anyway, for the most part. It was as if they didn't care. They would only notice us if we tried to rebel. So we didn't bother. And that's why I've tried to be a kid who doesn't stand out. But I fight if I have to. And if it's hopeless to resist, I surrender right away. That's been my attitude up to now. The only things worth fighting for are my own problems. The way I see it, the more people you get to fight for something, the easier it is to lose sight of what you were fighting for in the first place.

Officially, the people who are fighting for stuff are the kids on the student council. Proud of their right to talk with adults as equals, these people go around being sickeningly overenthusiastic. In their perfect school uniforms. In other words, seriously uptight. They've dared to deviate ever so slightly from the rules with their hairstyle, but it's such a tiny difference, it's just totally uncool. We have a secret name for it—the student-council cut. It looks like on one-thousand-yen bargain-cut day they all trot off to the hairdresser with their coupons. It's a style that doesn't go with fashionable clothes *at all*. Then as if this wasn't enough, they act as if school was the most important thing in their lives. The girls have surprisingly cute faces (and they look like they know it too); they're planning to use their looks to get on in life—even I get that. But they're sooo different, like when they climb the stairs, they always keep to the left and never loiter. Just in case someone might be watching them. Always on their best behavior and with perfect manners. Even when using the bathroom, perfect manners.

There's a suggestions box at the top of the stairs, but no one ever puts anything in it. Well, maybe the really uptight geek types do . . . But truthfully, it's not that there aren't any problems. It's all, "There are many problem areas in the life of our school, and it is important to try to solve these issues." Once a month—it's so retarded—there's a student meeting in the auditorium. The teachers sit to the side and don't participate. Well, they say they're not participating, but of course they're watching carefully. They certainly don't mind butting in from time to time. "You're the ones who chose your representatives on the student council, so you have a responsibility," they say. Well, I just don't get this responsibility. I don't want to have anything to do with it at all, okay?

The reps are all show-offs, anyway. And isn't wanting too much responsibility dangerous? I say nothing and let them get on with it. The girl reps want to be TV announcers or flight attendants. Their future is all planned out. They're taking the route where they can use their femininity to the max. I'm just not like that. We're not. When I say *we*, I don't really know what the others want. Akina and Namiko and Masumi haven't exactly said anything straight out . . .

What I want to do changes all the time, but there's nothing I'm really keen on. I don't *have* to do anything. No, I guess I'll do *something*. I'll live at home if I can. There's no real reason to leave. And I'd feel lonely living away from my parents. When it comes to pretending to be doing something, I'm pretty talented, so maybe I'll go all the way through to grad school. Then I won't have to get a job. If I say I'm studying then people will understand. (By *people*, I mean neighbors, all my school friends' mothers, and distant relatives.) I'm not particularly popular with guys, so that's a good way for me to go. Trouble is, I'm not that smart. My face isn't going to do it for me though (and I can't stand post-plastic surgery faces. It looks like they've just been turned into the doctor's idea of a cute face), so I'm stuck with relying on my brains. Akina doesn't even need to use her looks. She's probably going to go a totally different route. I can't imagine how she's going to end up. She's so *enigmatic*. That's what I like about her. Yeah, I'm looking forward to seeing how Akina turns out. She'll probably become a single mother or something like that. That's not so out there for Akina. I'd get to hold her baby. Now if Namiko was an unmarried mother, people would be like, "Oh, she's messed up her life," and look at her with pity or disgust.

In the end, just because we went along to the festival with Masumi, the architect guy didn't even bother to speak to her. He only gave her sideways glances. And what was with that guy he brought? He was sooo not hot. And the architect guy just wasn't cool today either. Didn't he have any other friends to invite?

So that was the night school building. I'd seen the lights on there in the evening. A college where you study at night, huh? Next door there's a hospital. Of course, that was all lit up. I couldn't decide whether it was depressing or reassuring. On the spot, I decided that I was never going to have a lifestyle that had me end up either at night school or in a hospital.

Every night Ryuji Toshima calls me on the phone.

"How can I help you?" my mother makes a point of asking. That woman thinks it's so funny to pick up before I can get to the phone. I don't have a cell phone. It's all, "You can earn your own money to buy one." I agree with them, but why does my Dad have to be all pompous when he says it? Can't he just talk normally? Actually, I'd rather have a motorcycle than a cell phone, and I'd rather have a telescope than a motorcycle. I really want to be able to look at the moon properly. But as I'm sure I'll get sick of a telescope really quickly, what I really want is an espresso maker. I've never asked my parents for one though. I never say what I'm thinking. If I try to, the conversation always turns weird somehow. When I'm speaking to my parents, all the words seem to come out wrong.

When I'm quiet around my friends, it's not because I'm ignoring them. It's a group where it's okay to be quiet. There's always someone who's not talking, but we're still holding hands. Adults look at us and think the group might split up. They say that friendship is fragile. That's complete crap. We just don't say anything mean to each other. We've learned that much over the years. The bonds between us may be stretched thinner and thinner, but they'll never break. They'll last forever.

So, high school . . . Well, obviously, I got in. I had to get my hair cut—school rules. Actually, it looks kind of cute. Think I'll wear pants mostly, outside school. The other three went to the local technical high school. Namiko's supposed to be quite smart, but she says she's not going to go on to college. As her parents are quite old (when she says old, that's only late forties . . .), she's going to get a job and be independent as soon as she can. Then after she's been married and divorced (she's already decided she'll get divorced—that girl has her whole future planned out!), she'll be able to afford to raise her kids by herself.

Now *my* parents are seriously old. Especially my father. He's fifty-five or six or something. Around there. That's weird. You hardly ever come across parents who are almost sixty. Akina's got married when they were teenagers, so they're still pretty young. Her mom remarried right after the divorce, and it seems all the family dress in casual wear and do outdoorsy stuff. I've seen photos. They make a really cute couple. But Akina always says how she's from a one-parent family. She's like, "I've only got one real dad. That guy she's married to now? To me he's just some man, to my mom he's the new husband, and to everyone else we're one big happy family." But then she says she doesn't miss her real dad, or even like him. "I don't care if I never see him again. I'll never choose a man like that. It's so shallow, choosing each other only by looks and not by what's inside," she sneers. I can't believe this girl criticizes her own parents' relationship!

27

Milk

How is it that when the four of us are together, everything becomes such a big issue? If there were only two of us, we would probably just talk normally about stuff. I've decided that if I talked about my life at home everyone would get bored, so I never mention it.

Just because we've started high school doesn't mean that we all have new friends, so, obviously, the four of us still hang out together. My school uniform is different from the others', but nothing else has changed at all. We're still very tight. Other groups have said to us that it's all just appearances. Whatever. How do you hang out together without appearing to, anyhow?

Anyway, there's this one guy who used to be a member of a group that hung out with us in middle school. He still wants to keep in touch, even though we've moved on to high school. He said he'd bring along three other guys, and would we like to go to the beach or something? I'd heard he'd bought a motorcycle. He must have got his license . . . So we're here. At the beach. We came by bus. I hate summer. How many times am I going to have to endure this season? Hundreds, probably. I'm sure I'm going to live to a ripe old age. I eat very sensibly.

Those four guys don't even come near us. We (that's me and Namiko—the other two didn't make it) are going to the bathroom in the sea. Every guy who passes gawks at Namiko's huge boobs. Then I get the leftover gawking. It feels good being looked at by a guy. And my rolls of fat are safely under water level too. This is totally cool. Depending how you work it, summer can be fun.

"This is awesome," says Namiko.

Hey, that's exactly what I was going to say. Not *this is cool*, but just that—*this is awesome*. It's going to be a blast hanging out with Namiko. We both want to do the same thing—flirt with guys. For a while, it is a blast, but pretty soon I start to feel pissed off being here with her. When the conversation gets stuck, there's no one to rescue us. Just the two of us hanging out—it's too stressful.

Akina being Akina, it seems she's hanging out with the beautiful, popular crowd in high school. Masumi being Masumi, she's taken up with the geeky crowd and joined the biology club. She's busy every day looking after baby birds and hamsters. Namiko doesn't really hang out with any particular crowd—she just flits about from one group or club to the next. Apparently, that works out pretty well for her. It's different from middle school, where you could never get away with stuff like that.

Each time we get together, it is clear that Akina is becoming a stunning beauty. Beautiful people, when surrounded by others of the same species, can really perfect their beauty. They are able to reach a mind-blowing level of beauty. There doesn't seem to be any limit to it! It's scary. Up till now, hanging out with us, she must have been holding back from becoming this hot. It seems she goes up to Tokyo and earns some cash appearing as an "It" girl on a radio show. She doesn't have to sell her body in some sleazy joint somewhere to make money. As for me, I couldn't make it doing either of those things, so I'll have to stay at home and live a dull life. Then again, I've only just started high school, so there's no knowing how things might turn out . . .

I didn't tell any of the group, but I'm actually going out with a guy from our class back in elementary school. Well, when I say *going out*, we've only had two dates so far. The first was right after my high school entrance ceremony. He called out to me in the station concourse.

"Komugi! Komugi-san!" I couldn't believe he used the respectful *san!* To tell the truth, back in school he acted like some kind of punk—always telling me to get lost, or that I made him barf. But when he said it, he used to kind of smile, so I guessed he wasn't really being mean, just messing with me a bit. Anyway, he asked for my cell phone number, and when I told him I didn't have one, he's like, "You're joshing me. Huh, you'll have to call me then." A week later, we went to a café together. It was the first time ever for me to sit across from a guy, or to go to a café where you did nothing but drink coffee and smoke. He never took his eyes off me for a moment. I couldn't believe how my hand wouldn't stop shaking. I tried to stop it, but I couldn't. I couldn't get the sugar onto the spoon and spilled it all over the table. He sat there with his legs crossed, smoking a cigarette and grinning. My fingers were trembling as I tried to hold the cheap silver milk jug. They were my fingers, but they were totally out of control. I was bright red in the face. Totally embarrassing! Suddenly the whole situation sucked. We've got nothing to talk about anyway. He's too much of a punk. It even says *Bring it on, asshole* on his cell phone strap.

"You know, my mom isn't my real mother at all."

This from Namiko, as we lie stretched out on the sand like fish on a grill.

"How come?"

"I dunno. My real mother couldn't keep me or something."

"But you look exactly like your mom!"

"Yeah, that's because her younger sister is my real mom. We're blood relatives."

"Wow, that's complicated. Doesn't it cause problems at home?"

"Not really. They told me when I was in elementary school. I just thought, *whatever*. If they'd lied to me about it, I might have turned bad or something, I guess."

At elementary school, Namiko went through a phase of pulling up the flowers we'd planted or throwing water at the pet rabbits. I decide not to go there. Wonder if she's got it out of her system now? So right here, right now, Namiko is making a move to deepen our friendship. But I'm in a total bind, because I can't tell her about that guy I've been seeing. The thing is, Namiko used to have a crush on him. On the days they did handkerchief inspection, she used to bring two and give one to him. Devotedly. "You'll make a wonderful wife," the homeroom teacher used to tease her. Namiko used to turn beet red. And not only her, the boy did too. But the other day when I saw him, he was all, "Namiko? Oh her. I couldn't stand that girl. She was always hanging round me. She had humungous tits too."

So now I can't say anything about him to Namiko. When he casually let drop something like, "Actually it was you I liked," I let him grab me by the arm, and we leaned on a random parked car in the street and kissed. It felt warm and damp and gross, but I pretended everything was cool. Actually, I just wanted to get home as quickly as possible. It was my first kiss. I didn't even think about Ryuji Toshima. At this rate, I might even lose my virginity by the end of the summer, because I don't really know how to say no. It's not that I'm exactly hiding it from Namiko, but I don't want her to find out. She won't understand. And I can't be bothered to explain it all. Come to think of it, I don't really trust Namiko. If I tell her, she'll make too much of a deal of it. She'll try to analyze every little detail.

This trip to the sea is really lame. Next time, I think I'll go with guys from my high school. Namiko's like, "Are there any decent guys at your school? There aren't any at ours. All the good ones are taken. Come and see if you like. There are some totally cute couples. It sucks, but whatever. You'll have to sort something out. If we don't get with the program, our big summer of sixteen will be over." I'm thinking of a couple of likely guys, but when I tell her that I haven't got the nerve to ask them, she's all, "Don't be such a loser! Give me their mobile numbers."

The whole thing's such a drag.

Later that evening, some punks on motorcycles turn up and ask the four high-school guys if they want to exchange their two chicks for the two that are with them. The high-school guys talk it over. I kind of expect them to refuse right off. Looks like it's wishful thinking. Namiko and I have a quick conference. It's probably safer to go with the strongest. And if we stick with these losers, it'll seem like an age before tomorrow's bus turns up. Anyway, we don't have any money left. It turns out every one of those guys from middle school is from a low income family. They're all the same. No career prospects or anything. Why should we keep paying for ice creams and float rentals for four guys? We'd started to wonder why we bothered coming. This time, we'll go quietly with the stronger ones. Then once we're in with them we'll just have to make sure we don't get raped. It'll be okay. I've still not done it, and Namiko's the kind who thinks guys' things are so cute she wants to tie a ribbon round them . . .

But it turns out in the end they don't even touch us. They just drive away. They say, "Careful with that fire" and stuff. We'd lit a bonfire, it being night and all. Suddenly the guys we came with start picking on us, and laughing, "Guess you chicks aren't so hot." A moment ago they were wetting themselves and on the point of trading us off to some random bikers. What's happened to those scared little boys now?

Mom and Dad have called me into the living room, and I'm sitting on the sofa. It's soft and great for curling up on, but right now I can't relax. I think I'll keep quiet. I won't even nod my head. Not even an uh-huh. What's the problem with that? Why is it so important to respond or gesture anyway? What's the big deal with that? I'll just let my parents talk. They start off with, "The world is becoming a more dangerous place." Then they're like, "We're talking about that kidnapping where the girl was saved by her cell phone." It turns out they're giving me a phone. Giving me a phone when I don't want one—it's like a mild punishment. And what's worse, it's pearly pink.

Don't they know their own daughter's taste? I guess they just try too hard.

"Thank you so much!" I tell them it's really cute. Why do I have to grovel like that? Is this going to be another way of restricting my freedom? In my life, I'm going to be exposed to danger, even die. It's going to happen. If it's my time to go, I'm going to go—what's wrong with that? Anyway, I'm going to live a long life . . . Fine. It's going to be a drag, but for the sake of my aged parents I'll take the phone. Truthfully, I'm not the type to screw around and get into trouble. I just hang out and don't do anything bad. I can't even enjoy myself unless I believe that.

During the time I've been going out with Ryuji Toshima, I've started to tell a few small lies. Ryuji often wants to cut school. He's in the twelfth grade at a technical high school. (He came up to me in the street near my house and asked me out.)

"Go on, please. *Pleeease*, Komugi-san. It'll be a cinch. You've got a really mature voice."

So I call the school and say, "Ryuji has a fever of 102 degrees. He won't be coming to school today." It works.

"Komugi, you are *awesome*." He throws his arms around me and gives me a loving kiss. "Can you give me some cash?"

He comes out with stuff like this so easily. When I look miserable, suddenly he's all, "You're so useless!" Ryuji is always surrounded by women. He says he's trying to do it with over a hundred women before he leaves high school, and claims he's already passed seventy. I've never really been jealous—in fact, I don't know what jealousy feels like. Unbelievable really, but I really don't feel it at all.

He asks, "Are you mad at me?" but I can't think why I should get mad at him. This is Ryuji, the man who has stroked my breasts, sucked and nibbled on my nipples. I wonder why he does that? Sucking, biting, and stuff? He's begun to try to get me to hold his dick too. "Komugi, this is gross. Look at it. All this fat around your stomach. You really need to lose some weight." Does he have to make that face? This is my body. "Come on, when you gonna let me do it?" This is another thing he's constantly bugging me about. "Okay, it's cool. I'm gonna keep on asking you, and you can just keep on saying no."

"Okay."

"What d'you mean, okay? Hey look, I like having my throat touched. This is an erogenous zone right here—could you try kissing it?" So I kiss his Adam's apple, and he moans and starts to get excited. Suddenly his pants feel wet, so I pull away. A sharp smell fills my nostrils. Ryuji hurriedly sticks a tissue down his pants. The tissue comes out with a thick, white liquid on it that looks something like milk. He drops it casually into the trash can. His mother cleans his room for him. I'd love to see her face. I've thought about trying to take a peek into the next room at this woman who does housework all day, but I decided against it. All I've ever done is call out as I'm passing, "Hello, Mrs. Toshima," or "Goodbye, Mrs. Toshima."

35

Milk

There's only ever been a faint little hello or goodbye in reply.

When Ryuji has changed his pants and calmed down it's, "Come on, let's do it. Next Saturday afternoon. Come over here again. Look, just for you, I've dumped all eleven girls I was seeing. Well, there are still two that I haven't actually broken up with yet, but I'm gonna real soon."

He had *eleven* girlfriends? Well, that's the first I've heard of it. "They're all really amazing, too. Some of them are my age, some younger, and some older. The older ones are the best. They buy me anything I want and let me do whatever I like. But they're so clingy. They can't hide how jealous they are." Incredible how he comes out with this whole speech, as if he's reading it aloud from some book! He keeps going off on these tangents, but we always end up back in the same place. I just can't explain to people what's going on in my life right now. I don't even try.

"Komugi, you are so cool about stuff. It really turns me on."

I'm going out with this guy partly because he pushed me so hard to, but also, on some level, because I think someday he'll be some-body. Whether he's a complete success or a complete failure, even if he ends up in the gutter, he'll drag himself back up, and he'll somehow manage to look cool doing it. Well, that's what I believe, anyway. I've never been blown away by his kisses—I actually end up fighting for breath most of the time—but if he wants to have sex with me that much, then fine. So I go ahead and agree to do it. And now I've promised, I'm stuck with it. All I've got to do is lie there, right? Then after that once, I'm going to break up with him.

Being with Ryuji is too exhausting. I never used to be this ditsy, but recently I've been forgetting to make a note of my homework, I smashed a glass beaker in chemistry class, pressed the wrong buttons on the vending machine . . . The list goes on. I need to get away from Ryuji and spend more time with my girlfriends.

"Yes! That is awesome! Yes! Totally awesome!" Ryuji is completely psyched, just because I've agreed to have sex.

"Our hamsters have had too many babies. Can you take one?" I had a call from Masumi, and now we're meeting. Since the architect guy, this girl has had no luck at all. It seems he got transferred somewhere else. We used to look out for him when we passed by his office, but he was never there again.

Masumi is far more occupied with the mating of small mammals than with human males. It seems there are more babies being born all the time. When I ask her if she hangs out with Akina at all, she acts at first as if she's never heard the name before. "Huh? Oh, Akina. No, I never see her. If we happen to be in the school cafeteria at the same time, she totally ignores me."

It's become really difficult to talk to Masumi. At first, I try to smile and comment on what an interesting life she's leading, but I end up getting more and more irritated with her. I say goodbye as quickly as possible. Then I meet up with Namiko at the crepe shop near the station. We talk, but the subject of Masumi never comes up. Akina gets mentioned from time to time, but only as someone who is moving in different circles, and the conversation drags. Akina constantly gets hit on by guys in downtown Tokyo. There's even been talk of her debuting as an "idol" singer. It seems these days she's going to modeling school.

To tell the truth, whenever Namiko and I get together, I feel like I'm yawning inside. I'd never imagined hanging out with a girlfriend could suck so much. When I'm with Ryuji, there's the fear that I might be dumped any moment, so there's always a level of tension. He steals motorcycles, gets so wasted he can't stand up, gets into fights all the time, and when we walk together, people are always calling out stuff to him. That's so incredibly cool.

"You're sure? You promised, okay? We're gonna have sex, right?" Under this constant pressure, and as I guess I'm not *totally* against the idea, I just casually reply, "Sure, sure." I don't really care for him that much, so it's pretty easy to give in. I guess if I really liked him, I would probably put more thought into it. Well, if Ryuji doesn't care that I'm so casual about it, I may as well let him have my body. Ryuji, sensing how I really feel, is kidding around, rubbing up against my lower body and gesturing. "Next time I'm putting this in here. I'm gonna pull it out and shove it right in." Why does he have to make it sound so dirty? Oh well, I guess I've made my decision, and there's no going back now. And probably Ryuji treats me like this because, on some level, he senses my lack of feelings and looks down on me. When I think about it, Saturday is coming up pretty fast. I'm really going to lose my virginity . . .

"I think it really sucks that you never make up your mind."

When was it that Namiko said this to me? I didn't reply, "Thank you for being so honest. I'll try to do something about it." I got mad. But I was afraid to fight back. Namiko scares me. The reason I'm still hanging out with Namiko isn't friendship or anything, it's that I'm too scared to tell her that I can't stand her, or how low I feel when she criticizes me. It makes me feel sick. If I don't say anything, Namiko thinks that she's sooo right and acts all smug. This is how my so-called friendship with Namiko just drags on. I really don't feel like hearing all about Namiko's home life or her first sexual experience. It's pathetic. I don't want to get involved. Gross ways of having sex, or how mean her parents are, these are things Namiko is good at telling. She insists on revealing all her darkest, dirtiest secrets to me. It's painful for me to even nod in response, so a lot of the time I just stare at the ground while she's talking.

"Later." Namiko gets up to leave. We've been hanging out.

"Yeah," I answer. I can't bring myself to ask her, "Are you leaving already?" I vacantly watch her go. Then I start to feel dizzy, as if I'd stood up too fast. I can't breathe. There's the smell of sperm in my nostrils . . . I can't think . . . What's the matter with me? . . . Nothing. It's nothing . . .

Namiko comes back. "I forgot to tell you. I'm getting a job after I graduate."

Oh great. Her bright, shining future.

"If I don't get a job right away, my parents won't be able to afford to keep me," she says, stuffing my leftover crepe in her mouth.

"Same here. My parents can't afford me. But I don't think I'm gonna get a job. I'll let my parents struggle." I force a laugh.

Suddenly we seem to be on the same wavelength, and for a moment I feel like partying. No! That's wrong. I shouldn't do that. But I always end up going with the flow. I'll just have to tell myself *this is cool*. If our friendship is going to continue, I'll have to be more positive. I'll try to believe that I want it to last. There's still nobody from high school who I can really call my friend. And I have to admit that whenever anything happens it's Namiko that I think of. I always compare the things I do with the things Namiko's done. I use her as a kind of life guide In my imagination, Namiko is my inferior. I have her test all the dangerous waters for me. Then all I need to do is jump in after her. Namiko generally recommends me to try everything. *Sex with Ryuji Toshima? Go for it!*

Right now I'm probably living a bit more dangerously than Namiko, though. I don't exactly want to be better than her, but then again I don't want to be worse either. Maybe I should have Ryuji and Namiko meet sometime. Then she'd be more involved in my life . . . I could ask her advice . . . No, that'd be too weird. When it comes to the love between two people, it's no one else's business. It doesn't matter whether I run to Namiko, or run to Ryuji, nothing's going to help me. They can't help me, so I'm going to take the plunge. Better to take a risk than play it safe.

It's the night before the big day. I'm thinking, tomorrow I'm going to go all the way, so tonight I'm going to try to get as relaxed as possible. I take off all my clothes and lie on my bed. My parents are sound asleep. First I turn off all the lights. I've just had a bath, so there's the scent of soap mixed with my own body smell. I lift up my knees and turn on a flashlight. I hold a mirror in my left hand. I bring the light between my legs.

So this is where he's going to put it, I think, as I carefully study the whole area. I wonder when it changed color? These petal things are too weird—they look like a drooping flower or something. I used to masturbate back in third grade, but I gave it up. Come to think of it, I don't think I made a specific decision to stop. It was more like that kid thing of being totally into something for a time and then getting bored. I probably found some new obsession. But it really does look gross. It's like there's something wrong with it. Tomorrow, when Ryuji sees me down there he's going to get turned off. It's okay if he hates something about my personality, but my pride would be hurt if he hated me after seeing part of my body.

I get a pair of scissors and start trimming the hair . . . Seriously, this is one bizarre shape! Kind of like a clam without its shell. It might look quite tasty on a dinner table. Maybe I should shave it too. Until it's completely smooth. No, but if I shave it now, then tomorrow I'll have little prickly hairs all over. Ryuji will spread it around that I'm all gross and dark and prickly down there. I wish I was like Masumi who doesn't have to worry about this kind of thing in her summer of sixteen. Akina . . . Yes, doubtless Akina's is a delicate shade of pink. I don't want to think about Namiko's . . .

Tomorrow when I wake up, there'll definitely be a blue sky.

Probably the most beautiful blue sky of all the blue skies in my memory. Maybe after a night's sleep this'll look a better color too I mean, it's the middle of the night. My eyes are probably playing tricks on me. At least that's what I'm telling myself. I'll take another look tomorrow morning in the daylight. I'll find out how much I can see. If it still looks gross, I guess there's nothing I can do. If it's a pretty color then I'll have a little more confidence. Whichever, I'm probably still going to go ahead and do it. How I'm going to play it, passive or active, I'll decide all that tomorrow.

First published, 2004
Translation by Louise Heal

Tamaki Daido was born in 1966 and worked as a radio scriptwriter before becoming a novelist. Her novel *Naked* won the 30th Kyushu Art Festival Prize in 2000. She was nominated for the Akutagawa Prize four times before finally winning the award in 2002 for *Salty Drive*, a novel that caused some controversy in Japan for its depiction of the unconventional love affair between a woman in her thirties and a man in his sixties. Daido's work is characterized by a cynical sense of humor and an offbeat take on female sexuality.

Inside

Rio Shimamoto

At the end of summer vacation, the night my family came home from Fiji, Mom got sick. We had just put down our luggage, looking forward to our first cup of green tea in a while, when she grimaced, saying her stomach hurt, and ran for the bathroom. She stayed there until the end of the drama on TV.

When I knocked on the bathroom door, only a low groan came back. Dad passed behind me on his way to the front door and started putting on his shoes.

"Dad, where are you going?" I asked.

He said that he was going to buy cigarettes. *Right now?* Before the words could leave my mouth, the door closed. As if to follow that, the toilet flushed.

Mom and I decided to take a taxi to the hospital. Outside it was just starting to get dark. As I searched for an empty taxi, squinting in the glare of the passing headlights, my vision gradually blurred, and I stopped to rub my eyes. It was Mom—doubled over and clutching her stomach—who raised a hand and finally managed to stop a cab.

When we had Mom examined, we learned her intestine was infected with bacteria, probably from the drinking water in Fiji. "We'll have you stay in the hospital for a while. You'll be back on your feet soon," said a middle-aged doctor with white chin whiskers. Next to him, a female nurse in whites nodded and smiled. The statement *back on your feet soon* and the words *stay in the hospital* failed to connect in my mind, only adding to my anxiety. But Mom put on a white, cotton, robelike thing and got into bed, and then even she began saying brightly that everything would be fine. As I looked at the three cheery faces before me, I began to get the feeling I was the one who was sick.

Outside the hospital I called home, but I had to let the phone ring for an obnoxiously long time before Dad answered. I reported the situation in detail. Just when I was thinking he would finally act serious, he said, "Got it. Now, you would really be doing me a favor if you could buy some batteries on the way home."

"Batteries?"

"Right. I think the batteries in the remote control for the TV are dead. You can't change the channels." For a second, I couldn't believe my ears. It felt like April Fools' Day—the kind of day when you're supposed to act calm, no matter what happens. I stuffed my phone into the back pocket of my jeans and walked across the empty parking lot. Directly above the white hospital building, a large half-moon was rising. At the convenience store I bought some double-A batteries, as requested. When I took out my coin purse and paid the three hundred yen, I found myself wondering whether Dad would pay me back.

Inside

Summer vacation ended. At school, I handed out wooden carvings of cats and frogs that I had bought as souvenirs. All my friends laughed as if they'd never seen anything so strange in all their lives.

"Just put it on a shelf or something, will you?" After making sure everyone got the idea, I headed to the classroom next door. Otori-kun was comparing homework with his friends, but when I showed my face in the doorway, he instantly left the group and strode over. One of his friends said something that sounded like a wisecrack, but the words didn't reach me.

"I thought I'd give you your souvenir." I held out the yellow plastic bag.

"Thanks. Did you find what I asked for?" he said, taking the bag. When I nodded, he examined the bag with a pleased expression, remarking that the words were in a foreign language, but come to think of it they *would* be in a foreign language. "Ha ha . . . what's this?"

Otori-kun had asked for something odd that was definitely not being sold in Japan. I had chosen a plaster figurine of a woman dancing, with a white-painted face and slightly pursed lips. She was showy, wearing a dress painted red and gold.

"Thanks," Otori-kun repeated, as he returned the figurine to the bag. "Can you come over today on the way home from school?"

I looked up at his face. Otori-kun was very tall, with broad shoulders—bearlike rather than well built. When he laughed, his narrowed eyes formed gentle arches.

"I have something to do today, so I can't come over," I said. "Tomorrow would be all right."

"Okay, I'll see you tomorrow after school. I'll go to your classroom to meet you." The bell rang, and I hurried away from the door. The moment I turned around, the hem of the bulky, gray skirt of my uniform flew up slightly and wrapped itself around my legs.

I said goodbye to my friends at the station, then went home, shouldered a bag packed with a change of clothes and Mom's favorite things, and headed for the hospital. Mom was in a large, shared room, reading manga comics I had loaned her and looking bored. She waved when she saw me and closed the manga, yawning, while I pulled a chair up to her bed.

"Did Dad come?"

"He came, but he didn't stay long. And look at this book he left me." With an exasperated expression, she showed me the cover. Boris Vian's *Foam of the Daze*, it said. "A water lily blooms in a girl's chest, and she dies. Your dad said that if I read it in the hospital, there would be a greater sense of immediacy, and I could really be moved. He never gets sick—he's got no idea . . ." Outside the window, the lush green leaves of the trees in the courtyard were still flourishing, catching strong rays of light from the sun and reflecting them in every direction. "But you're a great help to me," Mom said. She laughed as she opened the bag I had brought. I wasn't sure how to react to her contented smile. Finally, I started talking about the completely unrelated topic of school. "When are you going to let me meet Otori-kun?" Mom asked.

"It's no use." I raised my voice a little. "I've invited him to come over on the way home from school so many times, but he keeps saying we have to do this right, so we should wait until he has a small present to give you. Or else he'll say it's not proper for him just to drop by, and we should set a date first. I don't know whether he's being sensitive or just running away."

"That's how boys are when they first go out with girls. It's nice that he's being so serious."

I scratched my head. Otori-kun was definitely serious. You could say seriousness was his one strong point.

"It would be nice if he were at least as good-looking as Dad," I muttered.

Now it was Mom's turn to look uneasy, although she tried to laugh. "Say, Grandma came by this morning and brought a get-well gift," she said, as if she'd just remembered. "I can't eat it yet, so why don't you have some for me?" She pointed to a brown rattan basket at her bedside that was filled with oranges, apples, and other kinds of fruit. Using a knife would be a hassle, so I took a banana. A raw sweetness filled my mouth when I bit into it. As I kept chewing, a faint sourness emerged, and then the taste was just right.

From a curtained-off area came a rhythmic snoring so loud that it felt as though all the oxygen was being sucked from the room. Thinking it must be tough to stay on the ward, I threw my banana peel into the black trash can at my feet.

Inside

"Can I take it off?" he asked, and while I wasn't thinking yes, I said nothing and nodded. Large hands reached toward me and clumsily unfastened the small buttons on my shirt. Hot fingertips reached inside, searching more than caressing. My nerves focused on the miniscule areas his fingers touched, as though an insect had landed on my skin. When I looked at his face, I noticed tiny beads of sweat forming on his forehead. I considered shutting my eyes tight or burying my face in his right shoulder, but just when his fingers were about to reach my breasts, I instinctively pushed his hands away.

"Sorry . . . wait."

"Come on, just a little more."

"No, I need you to wait."

"I know, but just a little more."

When he said that, I actually shoved him back. Then I watched as he came to his senses, rubbing the back of his head where it had hit the wall.

"I'm sorry. It was reflex, I swear." I hardly expected that phrase to be my follow-up.

"That was so mean," laughed Otori-kun, taking his hand from his head. There was nothing to do but laugh with him.

"Look, I'm really sorry. I guess I still get nervous, like it's too early for that kind of thing," I said, picking up my juice from the table.

Otori-kun nodded. "It's okay. I'm sorry I tried to force it." He turned on the video game. The curtains and the papers on his desk flapped in the breeze from the open window and the whirring fan. I sat down beside him and picked up a controller. I tried to focus all my attention on the game, but I could feel the palms of my hands and the soles of my feet getting sweaty. Occasionally I glanced over at Otori-kun, who was totally absorbed. I liked the way his face looked when he was being quiet. His straight nose gave him a handsome profile.

It was last winter when we started going out. Otori-kun was in my class, and we had never really talked, but I asked him to a movie out of the blue. This seemed to throw him for a loop, but he did go with me. It was a Sunday, with some clouds in the sky, and it began to rain as we were leaving the theater. We got to spend hours talking in the hamburger place next door. I already knew that Otori-kun had a much younger brother, that he volunteered at a rest home on Sundays, and that he wanted to become a nurse in the future—but I pretended I didn't know and listened. There was just one thing he said, toward the end of the afternoon: "My parents have always been busy, so when I was small I used to go play at my grandma's house a lot. I know it's strange for a guy my age, but I still really like being around old people."

This, I heard for the first time that day.

I already knew from Otori-kun's appearance and personality that he wasn't the cool type. Still, I pretty much unconditionally liked people who were kind to children and the elderly. I knew that young guys tended to be slaves to their desires, kind mainly to pretty girls and people who could get them what they wanted. So when I found a guy who cared for people who had absolutely no connection to him—a guy who could actually say he enjoyed being with them—I fell for him. But trips to Otori-kun's room had begun to feel a little like a chore. When I was with him I really had fun, but the second things started to get serious, he would start acting like a completely different person. I couldn't change gears that quickly, so our childish fumbling was still very far from the real thing. I kept saying I wasn't ready, that it was too early. Otori-kun never tried to hide his look of disappointment, but before long the smile would return to his face, and he would sit there stroking my hair. At those times, I would wonder what was wrong with me. Why didn't this feeling of liking him ever connect with wanting him?

"You should just do it and get it over with. I'm telling you, if you can just get that far, you'll get used to it, and the two of you can set off down the path to true love."

"And I'm telling you, if I could 'just get that far,' I wouldn't be in trouble."

With a face that said she didn't understand, Ayako played with her hair. Separating one strand from the rest, she took a small pair of scissors from her red makeup pouch and snipped off the split ends. School had finished for the day, and ours were the only voices in the empty classroom. I was about to run some dirty blackboard erasers through the cleaning machine, but Ayako started complaining that we wouldn't be able to hear each other over the noise.

"If we don't clean up, we'll never get out of here."

"I know, just come over here first." Ayako pointed to a desk in the front row, next to the one where she had spread out her makeup.

"What?"

I gave up and sat as instructed. After blinking several times, as if to prepare herself, Ayako looked hard at me through eyes fringed with mascara-blackened lashes.

"I think you're scared because you don't know what to expect. Once you know, you'll have nothing to fear. Therefore, I will now lecture you on specifics of the procedure and mental preparation."

"I decline your kind offer," I replied instantly, but Ayako stood and walked quickly to the front of the classroom, where she picked up a piece of white chalk. On the blackboard I had just cleaned, she drew lifelike, naked bodies of male and female and began labeling them. Panicking, I left my desk and grabbed an eraser.

"Oh man, what a waste! After I went to all that trouble."

"It is not a waste. The waste is that you're so good at drawing, but you always pick subjects like this. That's why you get bad grades in art."

Ayako laughed loudly as she watched the drawing disappear. I switched on the cleaning machine. As I did so, Ayako sneaked up behind me and whispered in my ear, "Look, it's okay. Otori-kun is so impossibly mature, and eighty percent of guys who don't flaunt their manhood aren't that big anyway. You probably won't even have much trouble the first time."

"Ayako, that's low." I scowled in disbelief. She hung her head a little, then returned to her seat and propped her chin on one hand. I put down the erasers and went and sat down too. Pale blue veins crisscrossed the inside of the thin arm that extended from Ayako's short-sleeved shirt.

"I get it. I'll try not to stick my nose into you and Otori-kun's business. More importantly, how is your mom? Is she okay?" For a moment, Ayako's arm doubled in my mind with the memory of Mom's arm, the night she went into the hospital and they inserted the needle for the IV.

"They say she'll be able to come home in about two weeks. I never thought having to make breakfast and lunch every morning could be such a pain."

"You feel grateful when you have to do it yourself, don't you? My mom went on a trip with her friends over the summer. In just three days, I ate so much junk I got pimples," Ayako grumbled, pointing at her forehead, which by now was clear and smooth. I nodded, trying to look sympathetic, then stood up to leave. The desk where my hand had been lying was covered in penciled graffiti.

I stopped at the supermarket on the way home and picked up ingredients for curry and a box of ice cream. As I joined the line at the register with my basket, I realized I had memorized the layout of the store since Mom had gotten sick.

I ate supper and was waiting for the bath to fill when Dad came home, but he didn't answer when I yelled hello. I stood there waiting until he finally came into the living room and registered my presence.

"Hey, you could have said hi when I came in."

"I did, Dad. You're the one who didn't answer."

"Oh, really?" he murmured, rolling up the sleeves of his white shirt. He picked up the remote control for the air conditioner and lowered the temperature a little. I went over to the kitchen and started to reheat the curry. Lately I had the feeling Dad was coming home even later than usual. He sat at the table and opened a weekly magazine, which he must have bought at a kiosk on the way home. I couldn't tell whether or not he sensed me peering at him, but he didn't try to talk.

"Dad. Have you been going to the hospital before work?"

"I'm busy, so I really don't have time. If you have time yourself, it'd be great if you could go, maybe tomorrow, to pick up your mom's laundry."

"Yeah, I can, but still, you should show your face a little more. Mom will get lonely." My voice was harsh as I swung around to face him. He silently looked up from his magazine.

"She's not going to get lonely." He said this as though perplexed, then laughed. Not knowing what to say, I fixed his curry and served it with a small dish of egg and lettuce salad. Dad ate the steaming curry without breaking a sweat. I sat across from him, drinking cold barley tea.

"Isn't the tub about to overflow by now?" he asked. From the bathroom down the hall came the sound of running water. Dad speared a thin slice of boiled egg with his fork and brought it to his mouth, but before he could eat it, the yolk broke and fell to the dish.

"It's still okay."

"It's overflowing."

"It's only the sound of the faucet running."

"Just go and take a look, will you?"

I didn't answer. Dad stopped talking, scooped all the food remaining on his plate onto his spoon, and ate it in one mouthful. "Thanks for dinner," he muttered. He stood up and cleared away his dishes. For a while I just sat there, my hands folded in my lap, my eyes trained on the top of the empty table.

Every year during summer vacation, my family used to go to the west coast of the Izu Peninsula. Dad's company owned a lodging facility by the sea, and employees could stay at a reduced rate. The facility had plain, white walls, worn tatami mats, and futons so flattened by repeated use that they bore no resemblance to futons at a regular inn. It was hardly luxurious, but the three of us loved to sprawl lazily in our small room, looking out at the ocean. Every evening, my parents would drink beer and laugh about how the sashimi was still the only good thing on the menu, or how the lady at the reception had thicker makeup than last year. I would lie there eating snacks and cutting in on the grown-ups' conversation.

This year, before summer began, Dad suddenly proposed that we splurge. He said that company bonuses would be cut drastically starting next year, so we should go somewhere special now, perhaps overseas. I was excited, but I couldn't help wondering at this unusual decision.

In Fiji, Mom and Dad had just one shouting match. The sound of their voices coming through the wall woke me in the middle of the night. I could hear waves, and for a moment I pictured our old room in West Izu; when the wall of a log cabin appeared in the darkness instead, I got confused and instinctively closed my eyes. By morning, they were ordering the breakfast buffet as though nothing had happened. I never asked them about the fight. It seemed the two of them had agreed to pretend that everything was normal.

One evening, I got word that Dad would be late, so I made myself a supper of cold Chinese noodles, which I ate curled up on the living room sofa in front of the TV. I was watching a program I looked forward to every week, but the humor didn't penetrate far enough into my brain to make me laugh. Several times, bits of cucumber and ham slipped out from between my chopsticks. The house was quiet. The louder the sounds spilling from the TV, the quieter it felt. Just as I was beginning to feel swallowed by an awful feeling, I got a phone call from Otori-kun. Everyone at his place was out, so did I want to come over? I instantly agreed.

Otori-kun's family lived on the third floor of an old apartment building. The inside was packed with all kinds of junk. Stepping over things to get to Otori-kun's room, I noticed there was even more stuff lying around now than the last time I had come.

Otori-kun said it was because his friend had just been over.

In his room, we watched TV and ate some chips he'd set out.

"This kind of couple is really cool." There was a special on about a restaurant that had been in a family for generations. Otori-kun watched with interest as they showed the silent, strong-willed owner and his supportive wife. He was being so serious I couldn't really ask him to change to the quiz show on the other channel, so I said nothing and watched with him. The owner of the restaurant was forcing large amounts of steamed kabocha squash through a strainer. His arms were skinny, but his muscles stood out.

"I know what you mean. They do work they love all day long, and they always have someone they can trust. They seem really happy." I spoke with feeling, and Otori-kun reached out and put his arms around me. When he and I were like this, I always thought of the ground meat wrapped up inside a cabbage roll. I said that to Ayako once, and she exploded in laughter, so I never said it to anyone else, but this feeling of security, of being enfolded, surely didn't come just from touching someone. It must have come from being wrapped inside his arms.

Otori-kun's hand slipped around my back and gently touched my cheek. I closed my eyes. Then he stopped moving. Thinking something was odd, I opened my eyes just a crack. Otori-kun was staring at me, frustrated. I followed the direction of his eyes.

"If you don't like it, I wish you would just tell me. That really hurts."

I realized I had crossed my arms over my chest, taking a sort of defensive position. I quickly relaxed, but Otori-kun's hands came again, and instinctively I took the same position. Otori-kun bowed his head and moved away.

"Sorry."

"Don't apologize. For some reason, that depresses me even more."

At a loss, I turned back toward the TV. Otori-kun was also watching quietly. I shifted my legs a little, and my shoulder touched his. He carefully moved away. A chill I can't describe rose slowly into my chest, and I realized this must be how it feels to be shunned. We both pretended to focus completely on the TV.

When my eyes opened, my head felt heavier than usual. Yawning, I looked at the clock. For a moment I couldn't believe my eyes. I ran down the stairs in a panic to find that Dad's shoes were gone from the entryway. The clock on the wall, like the one in my bedroom, showed the time was past ten. I was always the first to leave the house, so Dad probably hadn't realized I was still in bed. In the end I decided I would just skip school. In truth, after several days of household chores and trips to the hospital, I was feeling pretty tired. When I thought about it that way, I relaxed, and suddenly ten o'clock felt extremely early in the morning.

I decided to make cheese on toast for breakfast. A delicious aroma soon filled the kitchen, and I sipped my tea and chewed my bread much more slowly than usual. Then I started some laundry and began to run the vacuum cleaner. Soon I felt sweat spreading across the back of my T-shirt. The sunlight streaming through the windows was bright, and in a sort of exalted mood, I decided that if I could just stay home from school and do chores every day, life wouldn't be too bad. I finished vacuuming the living room and the hallway, and while I was at it, I decided to do my dad's study. I climbed the stairs to the second floor.

Dad's curtains were closed, making it feel like it was still night-time. I opened the curtains and the window, letting light and air flood into the room, and vacuumed the hairs and dust from the floor. I stopped to borrow an English dictionary from Dad's bookshelf, which was jam-packed with reference books. When I took the dictionary out, the tightly packed books loosened up a little, and I realized a bunch of white envelopes had been wedged in at the far end of the bookshelf. Now they were about to fall out. I tried taking them all out at once so I could reinsert them. They were almost all utility bills, but I discovered one red card, which I flipped open without much thought. It was a Christmas card. *Please use this on a cold day*, said a message written in careful Japanese script. *Merry Xmas* was scrawled clumsily in English underneath.

This kind of thing can't shake me, I muttered to myself. I returned the card to the shelf, pushing it much further in than before. Then I closed the curtains again and left the room, vacuum cleaner in hand. For lunch, I fixed a packet of instant Chinese stir-fry. I didn't have much in the way of meat or vegetables to mix in, so it didn't taste very good, but I forced it down anyway. After that, I couldn't think of anything else to do, so I lay down on the living room sofa and watched TV. I wondered if time creeps by this way for housewives who don't have a chance to work outside the home. Stretching out one leg, I gently smoothed the white carpet on the floor with the sole of my foot. I wondered if right now, everyone at school was sitting through a boring class. I wondered if Otori-kun would notice I wasn't there. I wondered if someday, he would meet another girl and start to have feelings for her. When I closed my eyes and thought of Otori-kun, a hot pain filled my chest. Feeling the soft embrace of the sofa with my whole body, I let out a deep breath, and tears began to trickle from the corners of my eyes.

I must have fallen asleep; when I woke up it was already evening, and twilight was burning its way across the sky. I sat up, feeling that I'd slept the day away. When I went back to my room and checked my cell phone, there was a text message from Ayako, and Otori-kun had called. After quickly writing back to Ayako to tell her I was okay, I called Otori-kun. At his end I could hear the sound of trains rushing past.

"What happened to you today? I asked your friends, but they told me they didn't know. I was worried." Without thinking, I laughed. Otori-kun said something to the effect that he didn't understand why I was laughing, but the background noise was loud, and I couldn't make it out.

"I'm sorry, would you say that again? I can't hear you."

"You and I need to talk. Do you think you can come to school tomorrow?"

I winced, and pressed the phone a little closer to my ear. "Look, there's no one here right now, so why don't you come over?"

Otori-kun grunted, as though a little uncertain. Outside the twilight had faded, and in the darkness of early evening, the stars were coming out. A young man on a bicycle rode slowly by the front of the house.

"Okay. I'll be there in about thirty minutes." He spoke rapidly, then hung up. I tossed the cell phone onto my bed and looked in the mirror. It reflected a zombie with red, puffy eyes.

Otori-kun came a little late. I opened the front door the moment the bell rang. He was standing there in the dark with a nervous expression on his face, resting one hand on the handlebars of a white bicycle. Instead of his school uniform, he was wearing an orange T-shirt and cargo pants with a lot of pockets. A lukewarm wind ruffled his short, black hair.

Picking up a tray loaded with barley tea and snacks, I led him to my room. Otori-kun went in and sat down on the carpet. He glanced around, looking more unsettled than usual. A little nervous myself, I sat down on the bed. I wondered whether I should turn on the air conditioner. There was sweat on the back of Otori-kun's neck, so I did.

"Anyway, the thing I need to talk to you about . . ." He looked up at me as he spoke. I had stretched my legs out in front of me and was swinging them up and down slightly. I looked toward him without blinking.

"Otori-kun."

"What?"

"I . . . I know this probably hasn't really come across lately, but the thing is, I really like you." I was nervous and spoke much more quickly than I'd meant to. Still listening, Otori-kun narrowed his eyes. "So, even if you say you want to break up or something, of course I won't stalk you or anything, but I'll probably put up a fight, you know."

"Uh, thanks. I'm not sure what you mean, but it makes me really happy to hear that."

I slid off the bed and sat down on the floor. Now it was me who was looking up at him. "That isn't what you wanted to talk about?"

Otori-kun frowned, puzzled, then burst out laughing. "No way! Breaking up is about the last thing on my mind."

"What? You came in here all serious, saying there's something we need to discuss. I was sure that was it."

"No, no, no. But that was some leap. I kind of like that about you, the way you get an idea and run off with it."

I had been bracing myself for a struggle, but now I'd lost momentum. I leaned back on my hands.

When I looked up at him a second time, Otori-kun turned serious again. "What I want to talk to you about is why you didn't tell me your mom was in the hospital." Now it was my turn to be surprised. Otori-kun reached for the barley tea on the tray and took a swallow.

"I didn't tell you because I thought you would worry."

"Of course I would have worried. But you could have told me. I heard it for the first time today from Ayako, and I was floored."

"But it's not that big a deal. The doctor at the hospital says Mom can come home by Friday. I didn't think it was the sort of thing you talk about."

"But with a member of your family in the hospital, you must have been worried, right? You've been doing everything at home by yourself, and I had no idea. We're a couple, aren't we? I wouldn't mind if you leaned on me a little more."

Hearing Otori-kun's words, I began to feel pent-up emotions escaping. *Don't open me up too much*, I begged, but just to myself. As I stayed silent, trying not to break down, he stroked my head. That was all it took to make me choke up so much I couldn't breathe.

"I was afraid that if I told you, I would say what's really going on . . ." I hung my head and spoke in a low voice.

"What's going on?"

Before he could say more, I shook my head, then pressed my cheek to the warm front of his T-shirt. With my ear against his chest, I could hear the regular beat of his heart. He quietly rubbed my back as I closed my eyes and leaned into him. I could feel my body temperature rising, as though I was being boiled down slowly.

"Otori-kun."

"What is it?" he said softly.

"Would you make love to me, right now, right here?"

"Are you sure?"

"Please."

Even before I finished speaking, his arms reached behind my back and under my legs with unhesitating strength. He lifted me to the bed. Maybe I should have listened to Ayako's lecture after all, I worried briefly as I lay back. Then Otori-kun covered me, and his presence sank slowly into every inch of my body.

The morning Mom got out of the hospital, I skipped school and went to meet her. She let me take her bags, and as soon as she stepped outside, she raised both arms to the sky. "Let's get a bite to eat somewhere. Hospital food reminds me of temple food, and I'm ready for something else."

The two of us went into a restaurant right next to the hospital, where they had daily lunch specials. Mom ordered the grilled beef with extra rice. I ate my croquette meal and worried the whole time, half-wondering if Mom would stop and say her stomach hurt. But she quickly ate everything, then sat sipping her tea. She looked happy.

"I'm going to separate from your dad for a while," she announced, as she emptied her teacup.

"Oh. I was thinking you might say that."

"I'm sorry, sweetie."

"Nothing you can do, huh." I felt a little embarrassed in front of Mom, but I started to cry anyway. Would things have worked out better if we'd gone to West Izu, not Fiji? Smoothing my hair, Mom murmured again that she was sorry.

After returning to the house in a taxi with Mom, I left again to go to my afternoon classes. Climbing up the hill to school, I thought about how to tell Ayako what had happened with Otori-kun. He may look like he doesn't have much confidence, I could say, but you shouldn't underestimate him. But if I said that, Ayako was sure to get excited, and it wouldn't matter whether we were in a classroom or the hallway, there was no telling what shame-less questions she'd ask. Maybe I just shouldn't tell her, I thought, watching the crisp outline of my shadow on the asphalt. I stopped for a moment to catch my breath and bought some cold tea at a vending machine on the street. I drank it all at once, looking up at the sky, where tiny clouds were rushing past. Anyway, this time I'll be sure to tell Otori-kun what's happening at home, I thought. Toss-ing my empty can into a dirty trash can by the vending machine, I took off running.

First published, 2004
Translation by Avery Fischer Udagawa

Rio Shimamoto was born in 1983. By the age of twenty, she had twice been nominated for the Akutagawa Prize for her novels *Little by Little* (2003) and *The Depths of the Forest* (2004). *Little by Little* was awarded the Noma Prize for Literature, making Shimamoto the youngest-ever recipient of the award. Her fiction often portrays the loneliness and isolation that young people feel as they cross the threshold from child-hood to adulthood.

Piss

Yuzuki Muroi

Eyes half-closed, the old guy gulps my lemon-colored piss down his sinewy throat. The liquid in the Baccarat glass sparkles as it catches the light. It's beautiful.

Several girls come to this Roppongi condo at different times throughout the day. Somehow, they all look alike. They're all around twenty and are already tired of living, which shows in their faces and the way they act. But they still hold on to some dream of their own. Mine is to open a small restaurant with my boyfriend, Shin. It would be great if my dream came true.

My profile says: "Sophomore, English Department, Sophia University," which of course is not true. A real one would read: "Dropout, Kanazawa Women's Commercial High School, Ishikawa Prefecture." The profile also has things like, "Hobby: Handicrafts," and "Type of Man Preferred: Older, kind men." My headshot is pasted to the top of the profile. The Korean manager carries a stack of profiles with him on his rounds to get appointments. Since I'm neither a beauty nor particularly photogenic, I don't get that many customers.

If I don't have any coming up in the next three days, the manager asks, "What're you gonna do, Miyuki?" It's a drag, and I feel badly for Misa, who recommended me for this job, so I say, "I'll do a catch," and have him schedule me in for a temporary slot. This means I'm supposed to catch my own customer by the time the room charge begins. The catch customer commission is good, but if I can't catch anyone, he'll deduct the room charge from my salary anyway.

There's an old coffee shop in the basement of a nondescript building on the west side of Shinjuku Station where I can catch a guy relatively easily, because the customers there are all starving for women. A girl I used to work with told me about this place the day before she quit. That's where I caught Old Man Piss about a year ago. It was so cold that night my lungs hurt when I breathed. I picked him up just because he had this huge mole on his forehead that I thought was funny. When I told him I was a pro, he looked a little sad. But he was decent enough to take me to the room in a taxi just the same. Once there, he took off his grey coat and suit. Buck naked, he reminded me of the brown pine tree in my parents' garden. I haven't been there since my grandma died. When I got closer to him, he smelled like resin.

The old guy was an awfully quiet man. When I asked his name and how old he was, he just shook his head. But suddenly, he looked at me intensely and said, "I want your piss." I was totally speechless, but I thought this was much better than sticky, toadlike kisses, or one of those acrobatic positions my potbellied customers always demand.

A lot of these guys want to do a thorough examination of our genitalia, so there's a gynecological examination table in the corner of the room. First, the old guy gets me on the table and plays with my cunt or asshole using one of the tools we provide—forceps, and things like that. Then he takes a glass out of his bag, which I place between my legs.

In the beginning, I couldn't always go because of how he stared at me, but now I'm quite good at it. I never spill any on my hands or the carpet. He drinks my warm piss slowly, while he masturbates and ejaculates into a hand towel. Then he puts on his clothes. It's a ritual that's about as routine as a radio calisthenics program. We sit on the metal-framed bed, which is covered with a gold-colored sheet, and talk until the time is up, though it's really me who talks, while he grunts yes or no.

There's thirty thousand yen in the envelope; brand new bills like his starched white shirt. A tip.

"That much? Did you get your year-end bonus?" The old guy nods expressionlessly, but I know that he's shy at heart. "Thank you. I'll use it slowly. I'm saving money for when Shin and I open up a restaurant, but tonight, maybe we'll eat out . . ." He says nothing. "You're always so sweet to me. I'll definitely invite you to the opening of the restaurant. I'll put a 'reserved' card at the best table for you. I promise!" I'm not sure if he's listening to me. His eyes are already turned toward the tacky clock on the wall. Rococo style. That's what all the girls say. The buzzer rings. I get up off the bed to pick up the intercom. It's the manager. "He says our time's up.

Piss

Shall I book you for next Friday?" The old guy nods. "Thank you! I really like you," I say. When I cling to him, the old guy pushes my arms away. The word *Saito*, embroidered in orange on the inside lapel of his coat, catches my eye. "Is your name Mr. Saito?"

The old guy doesn't answer. He opens the door and pays the manager, who's waiting outside. I slip on my high heels and stand in the doorway, waving enthusiastically to him as he gets into the elevator.

Misa comes out of the elevator just as the old guy goes in. She's about the same age as me but looks almost thirty, probably because she's always getting into these stormy relationships with a string of different men, plus all the alcohol and drugs. She has chronic migraines and always carries a suspicious looking bag of meds. She looks a little like Julia Roberts. She's a beauty. She said she comes from somewhere near the American air force base in Misawa, so she might be half-Japanese.

Misa came to Tokyo when she was seventeen, tagging along after Shin. Before he moved in with me, Shin lived with Misa. I still get jealous of her, since she's known Shin for much longer than me. But I'm grateful to him for choosing me over a girl like Misa with a beautiful face and a good personality. He probably chose me because of my body. I like to think that I'm a lucky woman blessed with a good figure, since my face is nothing special, and I'm not even that smart.

Sometimes the three of us go out to eat together, even now. When we do, Shin and Misa have a surprisingly easy banter and joke around.

I know I'm stupid to feel jealous. The bottom line is that it's hard for Misa too. She doesn't show it, but she must be suffering.

When Misa talked to me at our English conversation class—I was alone and hadn't made friends with anyone—she probably never would have imagined that I'd be the kind of woman who'd take her man away. I would never have thought so, either. I was working for a small printing company then. I was dazzled by Misa in her expensive-looking jewelry and high heels.

Shin often came to the classroom to pick Misa up. Over time, he and I began to talk. He was very handsome, and he smelled good—animal-like—when I got closer to him. One evening, he came to the class to get Misa, but there was some misunderstanding, and she didn't show up. Since he was already there, he took me to dinner instead. After dinner, he wanted to come back to my place. By then, I was utterly infatuated with him and couldn't say no.

Even after Shin moved in with me, Misa's attitude toward me didn't change. She's so sweet. She's my best friend.

"That mole . . ." Misa smiles at me, eyebrow raised, as she points to the elevator door. "He's a good customer—one of your regulars, isn't he? He looks quite normal, though. Normal sex?"

"What? That's a secret!" I say, embarrassed.

"I'll make you confess. I've only got a quickie coming up, so wait for me at the coffee shop. Let's go for a drink. It's been a long time." She makes a gesture like she's gulping from a glass. I groan.

"Shin and I'll probably go out tonight."

Misa puffs out her cheeks. "It's always Shin, Shin, Shin . . ."

73

"Hurry up and get ready!" the manager calls from inside.

"Well, then, just tea is fine." Misa disappears quickly into the damp room. The door bangs with a sad sound behind her.

We are the only customers in the small, dark coffee shop. The gloomy-eyed barista is listening to our conversation with all ears.

"That client is the worst. He's short, got no money, then he just whips out his thing and says, 'Suck it.' I give it a quick clean with a wet wipe first, but yuck . . . it makes me sick!" Even though there's no alcohol on the table—just apple pie and black tea—sex is the only subject that comes out of Misa's mouth. The smoke from her Marlboro rises like a curtain, faint protection from the curious eyes of the barista. "He's extremely demanding! Telling me to moan louder, or to let him stick it way back into my throat. He gives all these orders, but then he comes so fast! And tells me to swallow it!"

Looking at Misa's furrowed brow, I start to feel a bitter taste in my mouth, too. "That's awful. What do you do?"

"Of course I don't swallow it! How could I? It makes me sick. I pretend to have to go take a piss, and then I spit it out. Can you even *think* of swallowing anyone's other than your man's?"

"Of course not. No. Absolutely not. Gross! Stuff that comes out of a guy you don't even like . . . Disgusting."

"Isn't it? If it gets in down there, then I can wash it out. But if it gets into my mouth, it's going to get processed through my body, right? I'm sick of all these pervs. They should put on rubbers and do it down there, like normal." Misa hits the table with her fist. The tea sloshes in the cup.

"Yeah, right," I say, stabbing the apple pie with my fork. "If they want us to swallow it, they should give us a big tip." Misa's eyes widen in surprise, which makes me realize I've said something wrong. The air suddenly gets tense. I turn my eyes toward the plant behind her, which is almost dying. The dry leaves look as if they might fall from the stalk any minute.

"Miyuki, you mean you'd swallow it if they tipped you?"

I brush my bangs away from my face. I feel as if I'm being scolded. "Well . . . I'd think about it."

"You're weird."

"I think it's sick too. But I want to get some money together quickly so I can open a restaurant with Shin. So, if the money was all right, I think I could do it. I'd just pretend that it was Shin's. Actually . . . maybe this is gonna sound strange, but can I tell you something?" Misa raises an eyebrow.

"Yeah . . ."

"Shin makes me swallow every time. Is that weird?"

Misa's face falls, and I instantly regret what I've said. I'm such an idiot. What the hell am I asking his ex something like this for?

"Every time?"

I nod. Misa cocks her head. "Well, I swallowed it too, but only on special occasions, like his birthday, because it didn't taste that great." She's right. It's not exactly chocolate, I think, looking at a fallen leaf at Misa's feet that resembles a chocolate flake.

Piss

"Ah! The great power of love," Misa jokes, spreading her arms wide open. The tension in the air dissipates.

"Yeah, Misa, as long as you think *gross, gross, gross,* it'll be a long time before you can offer your customers the love they need," I laugh, bringing the pie to my lips. For a split second, something . . . *the old guy drinking my piss* . . . crosses my mind, but gets lost in the rhythmic crunch of the delicious crust.

The phone rings. "Inoue-san, it's for you." The barista holds out the receiver.

"It's Shin. He must have gotten off work. I told him to call me here." My words trip over each other, and the chair falls to the floor with a crash when I stand up. I quickly pick it up and take the phone from the barista over the counter.

"Hello?"

"It's me. I'm off. Meet you at the usual place," he says curtly.

"Okay," I reply. He hangs up.

"See you tomorrow, right?" Misa asks.

"Yeah, sorry," I say, bringing my hands together in a prayerlike gesture. I take my wallet out of my bag, and place a one-thousand-yen note on the table.

I don't know why, but everyone hurries in Shibuya, even in the evening. From the window of the station's elevated walkway I look down toward the Moai statue, where a crew cut stands out in the crowd. It's Shin. He works at a restaurant in a big hotel near the station. He commutes here every day, but he's staring around nervously at the billboards like a lost child. Girls turn their heads to look at him as they pass, like they want to tell him something.

I run down the stairs, a bit disheveled. As he gets bigger in my vision, I start to feel breathless, and my chest begins to heave as though it's breaking into pieces.

"Sorry. Did you wait long?" I twine my fingers around his.

"Not really." Shin seems to be looking for something out of the corner of his eye.

"Shin . . ."

"What?"

"Nothing . . . I just wanted to say your name."

"You're acting strange. What do you wanna eat?" Finally, he looks in my direction.

We go to an all-you-can-eat shabu-shabu restaurant and eat so much beef that we have to loosen our belts a couple of notches. The beef is bland, paper-thin, and very different from the kind they have at the restaurants I get taken to by my clients or manager, but it tastes good to me because I'm eating it with Shin.

When we leave the restaurant, Shin pulls my arm, saying, "I want to show you something." We make our way through alley after alley of Dogenzaka, until we come to three old shops lined up in a row. The alley here is paved in cobblestones, like a street in London I saw once on television. My eyes are drawn to a pink cardigan in the window of the shop in the middle.

"That's so cute!"

"Let's go inside." A bell clatters as he opens the door.

"Excuse me. Can I see that cardigan?" A salesclerk rushes over at the sound of my voice. She takes an identical cardigan from the shelf and helps me on with it.

"It suits you nicely," she says. The price tag reads fifteen thousand yen.

The girl in the mirror looks so classy in the cardigan, I can't believe it's me. I feel as if I could even be a match for Shin.

"Maybe I'll buy this when I get paid next month," I say. I'm talking to myself, but Shin, who has been pacing around the shop, turns to look at me.

"Don't buy it."

I nod. "You're right. We have to save. Or we'll never see our dream come true, will we?" I turn to the salesclerk and bow my head. With a disappointed smile, she reaches for my shoulders to take the cardigan back. Shin comes up to me, blocking the clerk's hands.

"No, that's not what I meant. Your birthday's coming up, right?" Shin takes three one-thousand-yen notes out of his worn-out wallet and hands them to the clerk. "Here's a deposit." I'm totally astonished. Shin looks over at me, frowning. "Well, aren't you happy?"

I shake my head. It's not like I'm not happy; I just can't believe he did that. "It's like a dream. You bought me a present . . ."

"I'll pay the rest and make it yours on your birthday, Miyuki. I promise." For a moment, he gets this faraway look in his eyes. I drop the smile, since I know it's more than he can afford.

Back on the train, I notice that he seems angry.

"Are you sure you're okay about the cardigan?"

"Don't worry about it . . ." He's looking increasingly sulky. He has his male pride, so he's not going to back out now, I guess.

"Hmmm. Where shall I wear it?" I ask, brightly, trying to act as if everything is okay.

"Who gives a shit?" he says, then sinks into silence. I feel bad. I shouldn't have let him buy me the cardigan. I carefully press myself against him in a way that won't set him off again. He doesn't get angry, but I don't feel any warmth coming through.

At home, I turn on the TV. Shin turns off the light.

"What's up?"

"Let's fuck." Shin pulls up my skirt and tries to yank down my panties.

"No. Let me take a shower first." I try to crawl out from under him. His pants are pulled down, and he's thrusting his hard penis against me.

"Come on, let me fuck you." The light from the TV illuminates his pale face. His beautiful face. As I lie there on the carpet, Shin opens my legs and slides his finger under my panties and into my cunt. I'm completely wet. It feels so good, I get goose bumps all over.

"Did something happen?" I ask.

"No, nothing . . ."

"Is it something you can't tell me?"

"Nothing. Really." Shin's finger is moving inside me. I reach out for his penis and start to rub it.

"Shin, tell me. What can I do? I want to help you." His penis shrinks a little, then gets really hard. I want him inside me, fast.

"That shop . . . that clothes shop . . ."

"Yeah . . . yeah . . . you mean the cardigan? Don't worry, I can live without it."

"No, no. Next door to that shop . . . Don't you think it would be great if we could have our restaurant there?"

"Yes, of course. That would be great."

"It's empty. Didn't you see the sign?" Maybe it was vacant, but I can't recall. "One of our customers, a real estate agent, took me out for a drink the other day. I told him that I wanted to go out on my own soon, and he told me about that property. It's a bargain."

"Is it cheap?"

"Yeah, it's cheap. But I can't afford the deposit. The real estate agent is a close friend of the boss, and the boss said he would be the guarantor . . . but I don't have enough money for the deposit." As his voice becomes more urgent, his fingers start to move deeper and faster. I can't stop myself from moaning. "I saw the inside . . . there was a big shiny counter . . . it was almost exactly what I want."

"How much more do you need?"

"Two million yen. Maybe a bit less."

"So, let's work hard and save up for it fast. I'm sure we can do it!"

"We don't have time, dammit! If I don't sign the agreement soon, he said he'd rent it to someone else . . ."

"No way!" I put my arms around Shin's neck and go to kiss his face. His eyes are teary. "Oh! Don't cry, Shin. Money . . . I'll do something about the money."

"It's no use . . ."

"I bet I can borrow against my salary. When do you need it?"

"He said he'd come to the restaurant tomorrow."

"I'll transfer the money when I go to Roppongi tomorrow."

"Well . . . but . . . Miyuki . . . that job you're doing now . . ."

"Shin, please, put it inside me. Please. Come on," I beg him, pulling my panties down. Shin gets on top and enters me. I moan.

"Shin . . . Shin . . . you'll open the restaurant and wait for me, won't you?"

"Yeah."

"Really?"

"Miyuki . . . I'm sorry . . . I'm sorry." I put my fingers to his lips. He starts to move harder and deeper inside me. It's amazing. This is Shin. I want him to always be as wild as he is now. I want him to start up a religion.

He pulls out of me. I quickly shift around and start to suck him off. I taste my sweet-and-sour juice, which I don't like at all, but as Shin moans contentedly, I'm happy to move my head up and down like crazy. His body convulses, and I swallow the warm liquid that pours into my throat. A bitter aftertaste remains on my tongue. It reminds me of the taste of butterbur, a flower that grew on the hill behind the house where I lived when I was a child.

"Shin . . ." I look up, smiling. "Your restaurant's going to have seasonal specials, right? How about butterbur tempura when the spring comes?"

"You miss home, don't you?" he says, pulling away from me.

Piss

The next morning, I slip out of the futon, taking care not to wake Shin, and go to the office in Roppongi. I talk to the manager, who immediately arranges to get the exact amount I ask for, which totally surprises me. "Don't run away before you pay this back," he warns. Recently, there are fewer and fewer girls here because of all the talk about AIDS, or random police raids. I put the money in my bag, dash to a bank and deposit the whole amount into Shin's account.

Everything's gonna be okay.

I feel like dancing in the street.

I'll be twenty years old this weekend.

It's been a week since I deposited the money into Shin's account. He didn't come home that day, even though I waited up until midnight. I finally went to bed, thinking he was probably out drinking and celebrating somewhere. I thought he would just wake me up when he came home. But when I woke up it was morning, and he wasn't there.

I called his office. His colleague sounded surprised and said, "He was fired last week. He said he was going back to his hometown."

I wanted to call Misa and tell her everything so she could make me feel better. When I called, a message said, "This number is no longer in service." I thought I'd dialed the wrong number, so I tried again, but however many times I called, the message was always the same. *Shin. You and Misa.*

I don't know what really happened to Shin, or to Misa. I don't know because I'm an idiot. The only thing I know is that I can't quit this job for a while.

Harsh pink light from the neon sign of the pinball parlor seeps through a crack in the curtain and scornfully illuminates my face, as I open my legs to a man whose name I don't even know. I can't perform very well today. My moaning echoes hollowly in my brain.

"Uhh, the light's coming through . . ."

The young client, who says he's in the Self-Defense Force, doesn't seem to hear me. He just keeps thrusting his hips harder and harder.

I'm just a piece of meat . . . Better that way . . .

His sweat drips into my eye, and it hurts.

"Please close the curtain."

"You mean I'm no good? Quit complaining, you lazy whore!" He slaps me across the face.

"No, I didn't mean that," I say, but he doesn't listen, dragging me by the hair to the window. I feel weird when I catch sight of the ring on his wedding finger. He opens all the curtains and windows, and orders me to hold the window frame with both hands. It's cold, but I just obey him.

Tokyo Tower. Cars in a traffic jam. A city of neon and acrylic signboards.

"Show the whole city what you are—a dirty woman in the cunt business!" He enters me from behind and drives in hard. I can feel that he is much bigger than Shin. Despite myself, it makes me feel good. What a waste. On the street below, some women in pretty clothes stand with a group of black guys, their voices ringing out as they laugh and joke.

They look like they're having fun. I wonder what they're talking about?

Bathed in pink neon, I finally cry out too, my voice floating down to mix with the voices of the women on the street.

As soon as the man leaves, I go into the bathroom. When I sit on the toilet, piss streams out. Looking down through my open legs into the bowl, I see a scummy sea of yellow piss and white sperm, with a black condom floating on top. It must have come off somewhere along the way. After wiping between my legs, I pick the condom out from the bowl and throw it in the trash. I wash my hands at the washstand. I wash them carefully with soap. I feel dirty to have come with that guy's dick inside me.

When I come out of the bathroom, it's raining outside. I go to close the window, which is streaked with multicolored rain. We never had such horrible rain in Kanazawa. It always snows there. By now, it must be covered quietly in snow. I wish I could go back. I'd let the snow cover me, just like it covers the old houses. I knew Tokyo was never going to be easy, but I never thought it would be this hard. My eyes get teary, and my vision blurs.

Whenever I meet the old guy, I make it a rule to have a glass of white wine at the coffee shop downstairs beforehand. It makes me piss more easily and seems to make it taste better too. Today I piss more than usual, and the glass almost overflows. The guy looks kind of happy. He sips the piss and starts to rub his penis. He always ejaculates at the same time he drinks, so all that's left for me to do is pass him a hand towel just before he comes.

Looking at the old guy's darkened penis as he sits there gasping, transparent saliva oozing from his mouth, I think he might be pleased if I get down from the examination table and lick it. But I don't, because he might get annoyed if I do something he didn't ask for. When he starts to tilt the glass right back, I know he's down to the last drops, and I give him a hand towel as quick as I can. This time I'm slightly too late, and a bit of his sperm spills on my leg. It's warm. He wipes my leg with the clean side of the towel.

"Oh, I wanted to taste it," I say, jokingly. The old guy nods his head slightly. "I'll be twenty years old tomorrow." He smiles. "Shin, my boyfriend, he said he's gonna buy me a cardigan." He wraps the cloth around the glass and puts it back into the box. "It's a beautiful cardigan. We found it at a shop next to our restaurant. Oh, but don't worry. I'll keep on working here for a while, till Shin gets things off the ground." The old guy puts on his clothes and does up his tie without a word. Though we still have time, he walks toward the door. Suddenly I feel miserably lonely. "That's not true—sorry." I go after him, naked. "To tell you the truth, I got dumped."

The mole on his forehead slowly swings into view. "I could taste the sadness . . . ," the old guy says. It almost makes me cry.

"Pops! You won't just disappear, will you? You'll come to see me next Friday, and the Friday after that, won't you?" He nods and leaves the room. I sit on the bed alone. There's a pack of cigarettes and a lighter on the bedside table, probably from the girl before me or her customer. I light a cigarette and lie back. *Sperm is white, piss is yellow* . . . Talking nonsense to myself, I watch the smoke emerge yellow from my lungs and curl drifting through the air.

When the time is up, I leave the room. The manager is prowling around in front of the office. "The next girl got a stomachache and had to go home," he says. She's the one with all the sadistic clients.

"What's her client gonna do?" I ask.

The manager turns to me with pleading eyes. "He's a lightweight. He'll only give you an enema or something like that."

"All right."

"Really? Thanks! I'll pay you the same commission as you'd get for a catch."

The client is an old guy, about seventy. He's brought all the implements with him. He gives me a two-liter enema in the bathroom and then puts a huge vibrator up my cunt. My stomach hurts so much I start crying, and he gives me another liter as punishment. I can't hold it all in, so I let all three liters out in front of him.

The old guy is really happy. After he cleans me up, he sticks about twenty pins into my breasts, saying it's more punishment. Then he has me put his shriveled penis into my mouth, but he never manages to get it up the whole time. He tips me fifty thousand yen. When he leaves the room, I massage my breasts, which are dotted with red pinpricks. The hands of the rococo clock have already moved past midnight, ushering in my twentieth birthday.

Probably because my intestines have been cleaned out, I'm starving, so on my way home I go into a convenience store and put everything I can get my hands on into the shopping basket: pretzels, bean-paste doughnuts, chow mein, caramel, a boiled egg, a tuna sandwich, a curry bun, strawberry rice-cakes, a coffee-flavor jelly dessert, potato chips, Chocoflakes, a tuna box meal, some chocolate cake, a chocolate crepe, and a frozen cream puff. But they're all out of shortcake, which is what I really want.

It was Misa's birthday three months ago. She just beat me to being twenty. The three of us—me, her, and Shin—went to a family restaurant, and Misa had shortcake topped with strawberries. Now I want some too.

A clerk with dyed-brown hair scans the bar codes with a practiced hand.

Don't look at the red light. It damages your eyes. That's what Shin used to say, whenever we stood next to a cash register. I automatically look away.

"Don't you have shortcake? I want to have it for my birthday."

"If you can't find it on the shelf, then we're all out," the clerk says, without looking up. He reaches for the box meal. "Would you like it warmed up?" *Ticktock.* His heart and my heart work with clocklike regularity. Scanning bar codes. Fucking.

It's too bright inside the shop. Some people are reading magazines, some are looking at sweet buns, some are putting cans of juice into their baskets. Everyone moves at regular intervals, intent on their tasks, disconnected from the people around them. *Ticktock. Ticktock.* Like machines, moving with cold precision.

Back at my place, I tear open the food without even taking off my coat. I eat the box meal and stuff the doughnuts into my mouth. I eat and eat, but I'm still hungry. I finish all the food I bought and wash it all down with a Coke I had lying around. Finally, I feel a kind of satisfaction. I wait for a while, then rush into the bathroom and throw it all up. Now I'm hungry again. I look for something to eat in the kitchen and find a packet of instant chicken ramen. I break open the seal and bite into the dry noodles.

I'm a real idiot . . . A fool . . . I collect the garbage I've scattered around and put the futon down on the floor. I feel strange; sleepy but not sleepy, so I go to bed with a bunch of Shin's used comic books from his *Our Sprint* collection. Then I take out Shin's rice whiskey and aspirin. I wash the pills down with liquor straight from the bottle, but this doesn't have much effect. It's not until I'm half-way through the fifteenth volume of the comic book that my eyelids start to feel heavy. I sleep on the left side of the futon, though there's no reason to, now that Shin's gone.

Sleep is the only thing that is still kind to me.

It's early evening when I wake up. The manager is holding the room from seven o'clock. I've got to get a catch before then, so I change into my work clothes. I sit at the dressing table, and the woman in the mirror looks back at me like a stray dog. I take the lipstick to the mirror and color in the woman's eyes.

As the train rattles along, I feel the acid well up in my stomach. I cover my mouth with a handkerchief. When I belch, the man hanging onto the strap in front of me moves away. A woman in a Burberry trench coat sits across from me. She seems to be my age. She's reading a paperback and wearing ostrich-skin loafers. Inadvertently I look down at my own shoes—cheap vinyl, with the heels peeling off. I try to hide them by crossing my legs. *How do I look to her, in my fake fur coat with its bald patches?* The woman takes the ringing cell phone from her bag.

"Hello?" Just as I thought. Her voice is high-pitched and penetrating, like those steel orchestra bells you hit with a hammer. "I'm on the train. I'll call you back . . . Oh no . . . no . . ."

She makes no move to hang up. Her screeching laughter grates on my nerves, making me feel even more nauseous. A middle-aged woman gets on and holds the strap in front of me. She's wearing some horrible perfume. It's like they're all tormenting me on purpose. *I wish this train would get into an accident right now. I wish they'd all scatter in pieces.*

Next thing I know, the train is at Shinjuku. I hurry to the door. A wave of grey coats floods into the car. I can't get off. I'm choking—it's so hard to breathe.

Can't you see me?

I push my way forward violently. Someone's hands stretch out and grab at my breasts. When I get out of the car, I trip and fall down onto the platform. My stockings are torn at both knees. Tears fall onto the back of my hands as I crouch there. People look down at me, secretly laughing. They're all in grey, like my old guy. *But he's different. He's completely different.*

I walk toward the coffee shop at the west exit of the station. I no longer want to pick up a catch. All I want to do is see my old guy. That's when I finally realize what I need—a witness.

I'm turning twenty. I'm a dirty rag of a twenty-year-old woman, but I still have feelings, I still cry. Miyuki Inoue, who was clean to the bone, still exists inside me. Until today, at least. I don't know if she'll still be there tomorrow. I don't know if my heart is strong enough. Maybe tomorrow I won't care any more. But the old guy, he's my witness. He's seen me standing there, right in front of him. He's seen my blood, my tears, my piss. My purity. He never says anything, but I know he'll hold on to that image of me forever and ever and ever. That's good enough. I'll be saved.

The town is full of people in grey coats. *Everybody pretends to be my old guy, but they're not the same as him. They can't fool me.* I cut swiftly through the crowds, matching my step to the rhythm of the pop music that's blaring out from somewhere. When I turn down an alley, a rat runs in front of me. A big black rat. People say it's a bad sign if a black cat runs in front of you, but what about a rat? Maybe it's the opposite . . . Something good's going to happen. I know it.

I go down to the basement and push open the door of the coffee shop while quickly fixing my hair. There's a wall of cigarette smoke the height of my face. The grey-haired proprietor glances at me from behind the counter, without saying hello. All the ashtrays are piled high with cigarette butts. A customer is asleep in one of the booths, his face covered by a newspaper. That was where the old guy was sitting a year ago. My heart starts to pound. I take the paper cautiously from his face. No mole. I put the paper back over the man, who hasn't stirred. I feel totally drained.

"Excuse me." My stressed-out voice cracks into a falsetto, barely audible over the piped-in music. "Has a Mr. Saito been in? I met him here before."

"I don't ask people's names." The proprietor doesn't even turn his head.

"He's always in a grey coat. He's a really good guy."

"How am I supposed to know if a customer's good or bad? If that's what you want to know, I hear there's a good fortune-teller on the corner of the next block, up by the station. Why don't you ask him?"

"He has a big mole."

"Mole? I don't notice my customers' moles."

"Right here," I point to my forehead. The proprietor looks me in the eye for the first time.

"That guy . . . yeah, he was here. Just a while ago. Over there." He points to a seat in the back. There's a coffee cup on the table. I run towards the table and pick up the cup. Still warm.

He's around somewhere.

I leave the building and walk toward the brightly lit main street. I have a feeling I'll run into the old guy sooner or later if I walk around Shinjuku. When I think about the huge mole on his forehead, it strikes me that he looks like someone, though his face is not that special. Then I realize it's Kasajizo, the little stone god with the bamboo hat, from a folk tale my grandma used to read to me.

The temperature drops lower and lower. Clouds hang heavy in

the sky. I hold out my hand, but I can't feel any snowflakes, although just for a second, my white breath, escaping in a sigh, looks like snow. I rub my eyes. The streets of Kabukicho are a swirling, multicolored scrap heap of light and noise and stinking garbage. Roadside trees are peppered with signs and leaflets. Dead leaves shiver on the branches. *Who put these trees here? What do they feel looking down on this place?* When I look upward, a leaf falls on my forehead and lies there, like a soothing hand.

"I'm going to be okay. I'm still okay," I whisper to myself. I feel better now.

I pass by a restaurant, where a family sits eating by the window. A man who's about the same age as the old guy is lovingly cutting up food for his children. A totally different world, separated by a mere piece of glass.

Suddenly, the noise on the street feels louder.

Who's inside the window? Who's outside? I don't know any more.

Then I realize . . .

It's me. The girl in the street. I'm the one behind the window. The old guy picks me, pays, and enjoys me until the buzzer rings. I'm goods for sale. I'm a dish on the menu. I'm just part of the scenery. Here in the rain in the gaudy city.

Shrieks and sirens echo through the streets like mocking laughter. I frown.

My head hurts. Maybe I'm getting one of Misa's migraines.

I grab a piece of brick used to weigh down a signboard.

Oh, my head hurts.

I fling the brick.

It's going to explode . . . explode . . .

The brick makes an arc.

Crashing glass—what a great sound!

A scream.

Stop it, my head hurts.

Men in bow ties come out of the restaurant and grab me from behind, so I can't move.

"Bitch! What the hell are you doing?"

"Are you crazy?"

I laugh. I laugh loud enough not to be defeated by the noise of Shinjuku.

I'm melting into the town . . . I'm spinning . . .

It's the first time I've ever been in a police car. A young policeman holds my hands behind me. A middle-aged policeman fires questions at me: "What did you do that for?" "What do your parents do?" "Are you working, or a student?" He keeps his hand on my leg the whole time, for some reason, but I say nothing in reply. His hand feels sticky. I raise my heavy head to get a better look at him. His profile is in shadow against the headlights of the car next to us. I look down again.

When we arrive at the police station, they yank me out of the car. I spit on the shoe of the older officer.

"Whore!" The young policeman kicks me in the shin. I try to crouch down, but they hold me up from both sides. I keep my mouth shut in the interrogation room, so they take me to a phone. "Call someone who can come and get you." I call the manager. He comes in thirty minutes. They make us sit beside each other.

"You keep saying she's sick, but in this world, these days, just about everyone is sick. If she can't control herself, someone has to watch her carefully . . ." The policeman turns a ballpoint pen nimbly in his fingers. It's a different policeman from the ones who brought me here.

"I'm sorry. I'll take responsibility for her from now on." As the manager speaks, the policeman's pen drops to the floor. He picks it up with a tut of annoyance.

"And how are you related to her?"

"I'm her brother."

"You've got a different surname." The policeman raises his voice.

". . . Brother-in-law."

Under the desk, the manager's fist is shaking. He's angry. But I like how he lied about being my brother and repeat it in my head. He takes me back to the office in a taxi. Then he hits me. The taste of blood spreads in my mouth. I feel somehow relieved to be back there. It's where I belong.

The manager tells me to take some customer who's come without an appointment saying he doesn't care which girl he has. Customers like that are scary; some genuinely don't have a particular preference, but there are people out there who get their kicks abusing women, and any woman will do.

The man is like a beetle grub; flabby and white, with short arms and legs. He puts on a condom and suddenly gets on top of me. He has terribly bad breath. He grabs my chin and kisses me. I ask him to enter me quickly. He has a small penis. After moving around a while, he stops.

"You're too loose." He moves out of me, then pushes his condom-covered penis against my lips. It looks like a half-swollen leech. His pubic hair is soaking wet. It has my sweet-and-sour smell which Shin used to say he liked. I take the man's penis into my mouth. "Ah! It's warm," the man says loudly. Thinking of Shin, I finger my cunt. I get more turned on, so I suck harder, and the condom comes off. I carry on sucking. "You're good."

Shin . . .

"Suck to the root."

How are you doing?

"Move your head some more."

Are you somewhere where it's cold?

"Faster . . . faster."

Is it snowing there?

"Ahhhhhh . . ." The man shoves me away. Shin vanishes. "Let me in." He makes me turn over and gets on top of me.

"Please put on a condom," I ask.

"You won't get pregnant."

Why? I wonder, but then he muscles his way up my ass. It's my first time, so it's incredibly painful and horrible. I feel as if I'm being torn apart inside.

"Too bad I have to use a public toilet to do my business," he says. All my internal organs are being wrenched, and I feel like throwing

95

up. "Do you know how deep I am inside you?" I have no idea. All I can do is squirm in pain. "Squeeze tighter," He grabs me round the neck as he moves his hips. "Ah . . . that's good . . . squeeze tight . . ." I see a faint crisscross pattern of blood vessels emerge in his white arm.

Am I . . .

I trace his thickest blood vessel with my eyes to see where it leads, like some kind of puzzle, but I can't follow it to the end because my eyes are full of tears. My nose starts to run, dripping into my mouth. It tastes salty. My spine bows under his weight and makes a strange snapping sound.

. . . Am I gonna die?

He moans loudly as his hands squeeze me tighter.

I wonder if I'll die?

It's weird, but I'm not scared.

180.

The number rises up in my mind.

180 . . . what's 180?

When I open my eyes, the manager is looking down at me. I sit up. I'm on the sofa in the office. Oh . . . 180,000 yen to pay for the window glass, added to what I already owe him.

"Oh good, you're okay. I was worried about you."

I was naked when the customer fucked me up the ass, but I now find myself wearing underwear. The manager must have put it on me. The rest of my clothes are piled on the sofa. I knew he just means he would be in trouble if I died before he got his money back, but his words still make me happy. A girl who just joined the company arrives for her shift, and calls out hello as she passes the reception window.

Glancing at her, he looks at me and says, "You've had enough today. I'll reserve a room for your catch tomorrow. First appointment of the afternoon." He gives me a poke in the shoulder.

"Yes. Sorry about today."

"You're really acting kind of weird."

"I turned twenty today."

"So what?"

I stand up to put on some clothes, my head hanging low.

"So, shall we go out to eat sometime soon?"

I turn around, surprised. "Really?"

The manager is looking at his watch, not listening. I'm not particularly disappointed; I know promises disappear. That's why I'm strong. Putting on my high heels, I look into the mirror above the shoe rack. There's a crimson mark on my neck.

Good work today! I say to myself as usual, closing the door quietly behind me. I see the skyscrapers of Shinjuku floating beyond the emergency stairs through a veil of fine snow.

When did the snow start to fall?

I look at my watch. In a few minutes, my birthday will be over.

Happy Birthday. Good-bye.

I take a deep breath of cold air. Pulling my purse strap up over my shoulder, I notice a small box, beautifully wrapped with a ribbon,

Piss

placed in a corner just outside the door. On the wrapping paper is written, "To Miyuki" in angular characters slanting to the right. I undo the ribbon in the dim light of the snow, and find a pale yellow cardigan inside a layer of tissue.

"Pops?" Looking around, I feel his presence. But I don't see him. No one is there. Just grey walls, the same color as the old guy's coat, and the empty corridor behind me, stretching back into the building. He'll come next week. We made a promise, so he'll definitely come. I turn my eyes toward the skyscraper district and gaze at the red lights on top of the city hall for a while.

It's so sweet of him to buy me this cardigan. The same color as my piss, which he loves so much. It's funny, but as I hold the box, I can't stop the tears from coming down.

First published, 1997

Translation by Hisako Ifshin and Leza Lowitz

Yuzuki Muroi was born in 1970. Her resume lists beauty queen, actress, and bar hostess among her past occupations. Today she is better known as a prolific writer of essays and novels, and for her regular appearances on television and radio, where her outspoken views on current affairs make her a sought-after guest panelist on news shows. Since Muroi's debut as a writer in 1997, she has written more than twenty fiction and nonfiction titles. Her essays on love, marriage, and motherhood are particularly popular.

My Son's Lips

Shungiku Uchida

Now, a landmark's not that much use to me, Ma'am. Don't you know the street name? That would help. Landmarks, they're always changing, but now a street name doesn't change, see."

You'd think there was some special secret to taking a taxi, the way he's going on. I don't drive, never have a clue where I am, and there's nothing I hate more than drivers like this guy. I mean, why do Tokyo taxi drivers just take it for granted that their fares will give them directions?

"Sure is hot today, huh. How about a yogurt drink, kid?"

"Yeah."

"Say thank you."

"Thank you." I don't know why I make him thank the guy, when it's me who has to struggle to peel off the top of the drink in a moving car while I'm holding my baby daughter. I could do without this hassle.

"Oh look, now you've spilt some! Watch what you're doing!"

"Sorry, Mommy." But that's what always happens, isn't it? That's why I didn't want the guy to give him the damn drink in the first

My Son's Lips

place. It's strange, but ever since this so-called economic recession set in, taxi drivers are giving out snacks like there's no tomorrow. And they used to be so unfriendly before, these very same people. Surly. Rude. Bad-tempered.

"Yeah, I got a son and a daughter same as you—they're bleeding me dry. My daughter, she's on this study abroad program—she'll be home soon for the summer vacation. Those school fees are costing me an arm and a leg. My son doesn't seem to be able to hold down a steady job—keeps saying he wants to go back to school . . ."

Here we go. Get in a taxi with kids, and you get bombarded with stories about the driver's kids.

My little one pipes up, "Mommy, you know what's Convoy?"

"It's a gorilla, isn't it?"

"Yeah, but Toys 'R' Us Convoy, it's see-through and it's got red eyes." And here I am in the middle of a conversation, even if it is only baby talk, but no—the taxi driver still expects me to listen to him.

". . . and the yen's still strong, so they won't give scholarships to Japanese students. They think the Japanese are all rich. It's no joke, I tell you."

"Really."

"Mommy, you know Cheeta, and you know Wolfang? . . ."

"Yeah, she'll be home soon for the summer. It's nice she's coming home, but those airfares, I'm telling you, they're crazy."

"He's a wolf, Mommy."

"Just be quiet!"

"And you know those cheap airlines, well, they're not safe . . ."

"And they got Diver . . ." He won't be quiet. But it's not really him I want to shut up; it's the driver. The babbling old fool thinks I'm nothing more than a stay-at-home housewife, totally wrapped up in my kids, and then he feels free to regale me with his own superior knowledge of child rearing. It's so annoying. I'm not the woman the driver thinks I am. I'm busy with my job, so any spare second I can grab, I want to spend talking to my son. Even if it is only nonsense about toys. I want to talk to my own kid, not listen to someone else blather on about theirs.

"Mommy. Mommy!"

"And my daughter, just recently she's—"

"Actually, I'm talking to my son right now, so would you mind being quiet? I am a customer after all." If only I could get the words out; it would make me feel so good.

". . . but my daughter, she's a good kid really. It's my wife that's the problem. Tell me something, Ma'am. Do you put your husband's pajamas in the dryer?"

"Beg your pardon?" The sudden twist in the conversation throws me.

"My wife puts them in the dryer, and that jersey fabric—recently, jersey's a blend, right, a synthetic blend?—it gets covered in fuzz. Put jersey pajamas in the dryer and they look like they're covered in goose bumps. They shrink too. I can't tell you how many times I've asked her not to, but it's no use. She just goes right on putting them in there. Sometimes I think she's losing her marbles . . . She never went out to work or anything, maybe that's why."

"Mommy, who lost their marbles?"

"Just be quiet for a minute."

"But when it comes to my son, now you won't believe this, but she'll hang all his clothes out properly on the washing line, iron them all too, right down to his ban . . . his dan . . . his danbanas. Goes to all that trouble for those scraps of cloth, then there's me, busting a gut every day to support the family, and she goes and chucks my pajamas in the dryer. I just don't get it. And what kind of man wants his danbana all ironed and pressed anyway? A real man should wear his danbana straight out of the dryer. Who cares if it's creased?"

"Uh . . . don't you mean bandana? . . ."

"Most men carry a handkerchief, don't they? Don't ask me why. I guess it's okay if they're married. Me, I like a towel. Give me a towel any day—I sweat a lot, see. Now those I wash myself. And the rags and cloths I use to clean the car. It's all part of the job, I reckon. But when you're having a well-earned sleep in the comfort of your own home, you don't want to wear a pair of shrunken pajamas all covered in fuzz, do you?"

"I got Bomber Man pajamas."

"Is that right, kid? Bomber Man? Who's he?"

"My mommy bought the stuff, and she made Bomber Man pajamas. And she made my daddy's pajamas, and his are stripy."

"What's that, kid? You saying your mom's a dressmaker?"

"She didn't make a dress, she made pajamas."

"Well, that's great. When you think most people buy their pajamas these days."

"But the sewing machine's very dangerous."

"That's right, that's right, when there's little kids around. Ma'am, you're really something, let me tell you—sewing your own clothes when you're busy raising kids."

"Oh . . ."

"My wife, she could learn a thing or two from you . . . Hey, are you busy right now? On your way home?"

"I'm sorry?"

"My place is just around the corner, I could get you a cold drink, and perhaps you could have a word with my wife."

"Oh . . . no . . . really . . ."

"Please, I'm begging you. It's got to be fate or something that you got in my taxi today. People like you just don't exist any more. My wife, she's got no idea . . . but all she needs is someone to set her straight. I'll back you up. I'll even stop the meter. I'd sure appreciate it. Look, you don't even have to say anything. Just be there. Please? You'd really be helping me out." I'm lost for words. I can't think of anything to say that will make him give up on this great idea of his.

"Where we going, Mommy?"

"Now, kid, we're just going to drop by my house. Have some ice cream."

"Ice cream?"

Whatever next?

"Mommy, he said we can have ice cream!"

"Isn't that nice?"

His house is further away than he let on. He really takes me for a housewife with nothing better to do.

"Oh my! What's all this? You've brought home visitors?"

"We're only dropping by for a moment. Long story . . . We'll be in and out in a jiffy. How about some ice cream for this young man?"

"Mommy, what's a jiffy?"

Surprisingly, he has a nice tenth floor apartment.

"Oh my goodness!" His wife rushes round gathering up the washing hanging out to dry in the living room, muttering to herself.

"No, come on now, leave all that."

"But you know I wasn't expecting visitors!"

"No, leave the washing to dry like that."

"What do you mean?"

"No, it's okay. It's okay. That's why we're here. So it's okay. Hey, don't forget the ice cream. Make it quick."

"What on earth are you talking about?" She disappears into what must be the kitchen. Meanwhile, I'm still standing there in the middle of the living room.

"Hey, Mommy . . ." My son tugs at my hand. My daughter clings to me.

"Here you are now. Here's your ice cream."

"Yummy!"

"Say thank you."

"Thank you!"

The taxi driver's wife hasn't looked once in my direction. "Is it nice?"

"Yeah!"

"Really? That's good. Why don't you sit down here and eat it?"

"Okay."

"No tea? Aren't you going to get some tea for our guests?"

"Yes, yes. Tea, yes. Give me a moment." She brings out some cold barley tea. When I look down in the direction of my glass, I realize something.

"Uh . . ."

"Yes?"

"Do you mind if I change her diaper?"

"No, no, no. Not at all, not at all." The driver's wife opens a closet, gets out a bath towel, and spreads it on the tatami.

"Is that alright? Aw, what a cutie wootie you are! How old is the little sweetie pie?"

"She just turned one in the spring."

"Oh, it's hard to believe they were all so little once. You forget so quickly. Let me get you a plastic bag for that . . . Don't worry, I'll throw it away for you."

"Thank you so much." The baby stretches her hand out toward the tea. I place a hand towel under her chin and hold the glass to her mouth.

"My word, can she drink out of a glass already? Maybe she'd like some juice? Just hold on and I'll get you some."

"Oh, no, really, please don't bother! She likes tea."

"*I want juice!*"

"Stop it, that's rude!"

"Well, let's get you some juice then, young man. Just you hold on a minute." She brings out two glasses of juice. "Now, we don't have any little children in this house, and we've only got big grown-up glasses. Do you think you'll be alright?"

"Alright."

"Thank you very much."

"Oh, you're welcome. Aren't they adorable when they're so little? It's really the best age."

"Now this one here, he's a very smart young man. Knows a lot of stuff." The driver reaches out and pats my son's head. Nobody mentions the real reason we're here. Perhaps I should say something. Then maybe we can go home.

"Um . . ."

"Yes?" The driver's wife smiles over at me.

"I'm really sorry to just drop in on you . . ."

"Oh, no, no, please don't worry. But I don't know what you must think of me, with the washing hanging out to dry all over the place like this . . ."

"Uh, actually, about the washing . . ."

The driver slips quietly out of his seat. I'm nervous inside, but I feel like I can't stop now I've come this far.

"You see, the washing . . ."

"What? The washing? What about it?"

"Well, your husband's . . ."

"What?"

"His pajamas, when you put them in the dryer . . ."

"Uh, yes . . . yes?"

"Don't. He says don't. He wants me to ask you to hang them out to dry."

"Huh? You're talking about my husband's pajamas?"

"Yes. You see, if you put them in the dryer they get covered in fuzz, and they shrink."

The driver's wife brings her fist to her mouth and looks down.

"Well . . . well . . . I can't do that . . ."

"Oh. Why?"

"Well . . . let me ask you, what kind of pajamas does your husband have?"

"My husband? Uh, just the usual kind, you know, short sleeves . . ."

"Ah. Short sleeves. Well, I guess that's because it's summer."

"Your husband said he wears jersey pajamas, but that's just in the winter, right?"

"Oh no, dear, no. My husband insists on jersey pajamas, even when it's summer! He always sleeps in a jersey top and jersey bottoms. But your husband wears the cotton kind? With buttons?"

"Yes, that's right."

"My mommy made my pajamas!"

"You made them by hand? Well, you're really quite something!"

"Oh, no, no, I really . . . no . . ."

"Well, I must say I envy you. I can't bear them, you know, those jersey pajamas."

"Oh . . ."

"I've asked him so many times won't he please, please just wear normal cotton pajamas? At least in the summer."

"Doesn't he get hot, wearing jersey pajamas in the summer?"

"He really feels the cold. Only when he's sleeping, mind. And just him. No one else in the family. Complaining about the cold when we're all dripping with sweat. So I said to him, why don't you sleep in a room on your own? Me and my son like to sleep with the air-conditioning on, you see. But no. He won't hear of it. So there he is every night, wrapped up in a toweling blanket—looks like a caterpillar—even though it's right in the middle of summer. He's a real eyesore. But I guess we don't have to look at him if we're asleep . . ."

"Oh . . ."

"But those jersey pajamas he wears because he says he's so darn cold—when I go to wash them, they stink of sweat! His bath towels stink too. You think a bath towel just dries off the water when you get out of the bath, right? But you wouldn't believe how much his towels stink of sweat. He's sweating when he gets out of the bath, see, so the bath towel's mopping up all the sweat at the same time as the water. How come he's always saying he's cold if he sweats so much? He's so darn fat—you'd think that would keep him warm, wouldn't you? They say, don't they, if your body doesn't heat up, then you don't burn off the fat. But he doesn't care. Says he wants to hang on to his fat. He's stingy, you know. Still, a bath towel, I guess it's just a bath towel, but now jersey, that's a different story.

You can wash it all you like, but you can't get rid of that stink of sweat. I know the pajamas get covered in fuzz if you put them in the dryer, but I don't want to dry them in the room. He's fat, right? So the pajamas are extra-large size. If I dry those big, heavy, sweaty pajamas in the room, it only makes me depressed having to look at them. You're supposed to dry jersey flat—well, I'm sure you know that. That's right, of course you do. You know all about fabrics and sewing. So you know that if you dry jersey on a hanger, the hanger leaves a mark. But he doesn't know that. And there's no room here to dry them flat. He doesn't know the first thing about washing. After my daughter was born, I was laid up in bed for while. I had difficult births with both my son and my daughter, you know—ended up having a caesarean with her. Anyway, when I was laid up, he washed the baby clothes for me. All well and good, but what did he go and do but hang them out to dry on these big, thick, black, men's coat hangers! How he stretched those tiny little clothes over them in the first place, I'll never know. I was appalled. From then on, I've always known, when it comes to washing, best just to leave it all to me. And another thing about him—no sense of smell. He can't tell if clothes smell bad and need washing. And food? He doesn't know if it's gone off unless he looks at the sell-by date or brings it to me so I can tell him. I think it's his bad sense of smell makes him overeat. That's why he's so fat. It's hard to appreciate food without a sense of smell, so he doesn't feel satisfied unless he stuffs himself. My son, now he's very slim. And me, well, I've put weight on too, so I guess he doesn't look like either of us, but they're all so skinny the young

My Son's Lips

people nowadays, aren't they? I'm always telling him to eat more, but he doesn't have much appetite. Always been a poor eater, ever since he was a child. That's how I got so fat—finishing off his leftovers every day. Isn't that right, little boy? You're nice and slim now, aren't you? Is your daddy slim too?"

"My daddy's a big fatty."

"Well, that's men for you. They only eat fattening things. I try out those healthy recipes you see on TV, but my son's the only one who'll eat them. My husband says he can't go to work on that rabbit food. Always going for a bowl of ramen in the middle of the night. That's the thing about taxi drivers. They know all the special little all-night places. He's so proud of the fact—always offering to show our son all these great cafés that no one else knows about. But our son isn't interested. The young generation couldn't care less about eating. It used to bother me when he left his food, and there was nothing I could do about it. Now, I've got used to it. That's just how it is. And that kid, he's not just healthy, he's slim and trim too. We should be taking a leaf out of his book. I've told his father, but of course he doesn't like the sound of that . . . ha!"

"Oh . . ."

"So I usually end up making deep-fried food, if that's what it takes to keep him happy. My son eats it too. Well, he'll eat it, but he never finishes it all. And I end up eating all the leftovers, so I just can't shift these extra pounds. You can't freeze deep-fried food, you see. They sell it frozen, don't they, but I don't think those frozen pork cutlets taste so good, do you?"

"Mmmm. Not really . . ."

"Do you make fried food yourself then? You're so slim and stylish, even though you're bringing up two little ones. Are you on a diet?"

"Oh, no . . . not really . . ."

"But you don't eat fried food . . ."

"Well, not so much . . ."

"That's right, that's right. And recently everyone's bothered about the smell of oil, aren't they? They do that oil with no smell now. Whatever will they think of next? And then, did you know, you can make soap out of leftover oil? If we did that, our house would be full of soap! He could give up the taxi driving, and we could open a soap shop! Ha!"

"Do you have to make lots and lots of soap?" my son chimes in. "Because I made soap . . ."

"You made soap, did you, little boy?"

"I made soap with my mommy. But if you only make one, you can't be a shop, can you?"

"No, that's right. Well, you sure are handy, making all these things!"

"Oh, no, no. It was only a kindergarten project."

"Ah, yes, they make the boys do home economics these days, don't they? They don't just let them do woodwork any more. Our son's a very good cook. Our daughter doesn't bother so much, but now and then he makes us a meal. He really loves cooking. He's so good, he could go into business. I'm all thumbs in the kitchen, but that boy can do anything."

"*I* can do anything."

"Yes, you're a very clever boy, aren't you? And the washing . . . I was brought up in the country, and we always used to hang the washing up outside. But here, we're on the tenth floor, and the wind is so strong, you can't take your eyes off the things for a minute in case they're blown away. Well, nothing's actually blown away yet, but sometimes things fall off onto the floor of the balcony. They get covered in dirt. I do my best to keep that balcony clean, but the wind blows in all this grit and grime. Now, little boy, here's a question for you. What do you think the wind blows on to the balcony at this time of year? Cicadas! That's right, cicadas! If you open the window, all these dead cicadas blow in. Just the thought of it gives me the shivers. You can't put the futons or the blankets out to air without worrying about it. It's my husband who likes living so high up. I hate it! I really hate it. You wouldn't believe how frightening it is when there's an earthquake. He says we're safer up here than in a house down on the ground, but you never know with earthquakes, do you? It sways like crazy up here. Feels like it's the end of the world, even when it's just a small tremor. And it doesn't matter how strong the building is, if the big one comes, I know I'm going to die of a heart attack. Why he loves high places so much, I don't know. Even when we go on holiday, all he wants to do is go up towers, ride cable cars . . . Lately, I leave him to it. I tell him I'll see him later and go off and do some gift shopping."

"Mmm. Yes."

"And you know, when it comes to the children, you've just got to let them do what they want to do. Let them learn a trade. That's why we let my daughter go study overseas. That's what all the young girls seem to be doing these days. Now, if my son said he was going, then I'd be sad. But that kid likes to take things slow. He goes at his own pace, and as long as my husband is healthy and working, I think the boy should take his time and think about what he wants to do. Everyone's in such a hurry to get a job these days, but these big companies, they're all folding. You can't tell which one's going to go under next. I don't say this in front of my husband, but between you and me, I never dreamed I'd end up with a taxi driver! Really though, if you think about it, compared to some guy who's been dumped by the company he was relying on to take care of him, well, there's always money in taxis, isn't there? Ha! Well, it's true isn't it? Let's be honest here. But even the taxis are getting fewer customers these days. It's terrible. I wouldn't want to let our son do it. He's the happy-go-lucky sort. He'd probably let drunks in his taxi because he's softhearted, and then he wouldn't know how to deal with them, and I dread to think what would happen. It might suit my daughter though. You see more women taxi drivers these days, don't you? I guess if you can speak English you can be a guide for people from other countries. My daughter went a little bit wild in junior high. Ha! She was really trouble by the time she got to high school. Said she wanted to drop out. She always had good grades though, so it would have been a shame. That's why we sent her abroad. She's fluent in English now. And her father's so pleased that he can learn English from her. He doesn't need to go to one of those English

My Son's Lips

language schools . . . Don't know if he was ever planning on going though, to tell you the truth."

"Hey," the driver says from the hallway. "Don't you be holding them up now."

"Oh, no, no. Shouldn't hold you up. Now then, little boy, make sure you come visit again some time."

"Yes," my son replies. But there's no way we're ever coming back here again.

"Sorry about that," says the driver as we zoom off. He's stopped the meter but he still charges me the taxi fare. I step out of the cab exhausted, weighed down with my sleeping daughter and heavy bags. At last we get inside the house, and I switch on the air-conditioning. It's still so hot you wouldn't think it was evening. My living room seems cramped after the taxi driver's spacious apartment. How can they afford it when the daughter's studying abroad, the son doesn't work, and she's just a stay-at-home housewife? Rolling around in that huge apartment, the pair of them so fat!

"But happy, I guess," I say out loud.

"You happy, Mommy?" asks my son.

"I'm not talking about me, I'm talking about that taxi driver."

"Are we going to go see them again?"

"No, we're not."

"We're not?"

"No way."

"Why?"

"Because we're not, that's why. Okay, quickly, socks off, and put them in the washing machine."

"Can we put my socks in the dryer?"

"Mmm . . . not sure. Show me."

"Show you what?"

"Your socks. Oh, these socks, yes, it's okay to put them in the dryer."

"Is it?"

"But we can't put the green ones with the stars in. Or the panda ones."

"Why?"

"Because they're synthetic. If you put them in they'll get covered in fluff."

"Oh . . ."

"Okay, let's get started with the dinner. What should we have?"

"Things *I* like!"

"That's enough of that kind of talk!"

"If it's all *my* favorite stuff, I'll eat it all up."

"I'm asking you to speak properly and tell me the names of the food you want to eat!" I say. But I only buy the food my son likes anyway.

"Uh, today . . ."

"What?"

I can't decide whether to tell my husband. "We went to this stranger's house . . ."

"A stranger's house? What for?"

"I had ice cream at the driver's house!" When he hears my son say this, my husband finally manages to remove his gaze from the TV screen.

"Driver? What driver?"

"The taxi driver."

"What? Is he someone you know?"

"I just said it was a stranger's house, didn't I?"

"What were you doing, going to the house of a taxi driver you don't even know?"

"He asked me to."

"Why did he ask you to?"

"He wanted me to give his wife some advice."

"What? You mean like counseling?"

"Well, no, not really, just . . . just . . ."

"What, she has no friends or something?"

"Well, no . . . I'm not sure what he wanted . . . He asked me to go, so I just did."

"So you just did? You just took our kids to a stranger's house? Isn't that a bit weird?"

"Yeah, I know, but . . ."

"What if something had happened . . . ?"

"Nothing did. It was okay."

"But these were strangers, right? That's crazy."

"Yeah, I know, but it was difficult . . . It was a hundred times easier just to go, rather than refuse him . . ."

"What, he thought you had time on your hands or something?"

"Yes. Yes! That's exactly right! You know, I'm so spaced out these days, and when he took me for some housewife with too much free time on her hands, I believed him! Yes . . . that's it!"

My husband appears speechless with disgust. The baby looks from my face to his face and back again. My son has lost interest and is absorbed in his toys.

A few days later, I'm out on a work appointment in the same neighborhood as the taxi driver's apartment block. I just know the building is close by, but although I look really hard, I can't see it.

Then it's a few days after that. I don't know how often I've asked them not to, but yet again they've assigned me this young, male, junior member of staff to look after.

"This one's probably okay. It won't be like all the other times." I'm not quite sure what the boss means.

"Well, I really don't think I can do it. If I think it's not working out, I want you to give him to someone else."

"And who's going to decide if it's working out or not?"

"Me, of course. I can tell by now, you know, whether it's going to work out."

"Well, we do hope you'll give it your best shot. Maybe you need to look at your own attitude too . . ."

"So people have been talking about me?"

"No, that's not what I meant."

"Very well. I'll do my best." It's always ended in failure with the boys they've given me up to now; they start behaving like spoilt children around me, and then they're all hurt when I get them transferred to another department. When they find out I have a small son, it's as if they suddenly see me as their mother. They act as if I should be happy to have such a cute young subordinate. Why is that? You are not my son. Things can be going really well, but one word of criticism from me, and they wait until there's no one around then start looking at me with a sulky expression as if they think they're James Dean. *You scolded me.* And even though they're taller than me, they somehow cleverly manage to look up at me from under furrowed brows. I'm sick of it. That face. I'm really losing enthusiasm for the job. "This is a workplace you know," I tell them. "Yes. I did the very best I could," they say, biting their lip, in a performance that wouldn't fool an elementary school teacher. "Well, I'm sorry, I'm going to have to move you to another section."

When they ask me to take on one of these boys, it's difficult to explain why I don't want to. They just form a dependence on me, as if it was the natural thing to do. Everyone seems to see me as this indulgent type. Sometimes, I lose all my self-confidence and start to worry that maybe I am that indulgent type. Perhaps my son will grow up to be one of these ridiculous, face-pulling young men. The thought depresses me. If these are the only junior members of staff they can find, I'd rather work alone.

"Thank you. I'm looking forward to working here."

He bows properly, with both hands at his side. He's a good kid—really pays attention to the small things. Knows how to make a good impression. But there's lots of them who do quite well as far as this kind of thing is concerned. So this time, I've been thinking. It's got to be my fault. I'm taking care of my son and my daughter every day, cuddling them, having nonsense conversations, dressing them, bathing them—doubtless giving off the sweet smell of all that close contact when I come to work. I leave work early to go to my son's kindergarten events, I take time off when my daughter is sick. I think I switch off from all that stuff when I'm at the office, but in reality I'm completely out of step with my coworkers. This time I'll be careful to keep my distance from the boy. I really will.

But I can't get away from the fact that this one seems like a good kid. We sit next to each other at the welcome party and end up talking to each other. Then after the party, we find ourselves walking in the same direction. Maybe it's not such a good idea to be seen going off together. He's probably been warned about the boss lady by people who think they're doing him a favor. I do my best to switch back into workplace mode as we walk through the evening streets. I look at my watch. "Oh no! I think I'd better jump in a cab."

"Oh, yes, fine. I'm very sorry to have kept you."

"Can I drop you off somewhere?" I say, speaking as his boss.

I tell the taxi driver our destination, and when he replies I feel a terrible foreboding at the sound of his voice. It can't be. No. No way. I mean, I couldn't even find his apartment block again. It was so hot that day, it was just a mirage that my son and I saw, wasn't it? Or maybe it was only me. I was the one who saw the mirage. And my son just went along with whatever I said.

"Are you okay?" asks the boy, seeming worried by my silence.

"Yes, yes, I'm fine." My reply is brisk and businesslike, but for some reason my lips are moving towards his and then touching them. He doesn't seem surprised and just lets me do it. I open my eyes and glance from the boy to the driver, then back to the boy again. His lips are as soft as a baby's cheek.

First published, 2000

Translation by Cathy Layne

Shungiku Uchida was born in 1959. She shocked Japan with the publication of her novel *Father Fucker* (1993), a hard-hitting story of domestic sexual abuse, but she is perhaps best known as a manga artist. Uchida is also an actress, winning critical acclaim for her performance as the mother in cult director Takashi Miike's *Visitor Q*.

Her Room

Chiya Fujino

The reason Kyoko went to visit Kitahara-san was because the woman herself invited her. She had made the invitation during a phone call one evening.

"Uh, yeah . . . ," Kyoko had replied, not wishing to seem disagreeable, although she didn't really have any intention of going. For one thing, she'd only ever met her three times, and each of those times had been with other people, or with a large group at dinner. She couldn't remember the two of them talking up a storm about anything, or particularly hitting it off. And it wasn't as if they lived near each other or even on the same side of town; so despite Kitahara-san's insistent tone, surely it couldn't be a serious invitation. Or so she thought.

But she was wrong.

When? When? When? When? All of a sudden, Kitahara-san was pressing her for an answer. Kyoko was honestly quite taken aback. What had got into the woman?

"Well, it's kind of difficult to say exactly when . . . ," replied

Kyoko, hoping that her hesitation would be a tactful way of putting things off for a while. She was the kind of person who was good at getting her point across without rocking the boat, and if she was being pressured into something she wanted to get out of, a vague half answer usually did the trick. But the telephone calls kept coming with the same persistent invitation, and Kyoko realized that vague half answers weren't going to cut it this time.

"But we hardly know each other!" By about the fourth phone call, Kyoko was getting pretty exasperated, but Kitahara-san didn't seem to notice.

"Come on over, and I'll fix you one of my homemade dishes," she insisted, in her strangely cloying voice. You'd think she was a top chef, the way she was going on, but Kyoko remembered her saying once that she'd hardly ever cooked anything in her life.

"As if I'd want to eat anything you made!" She felt so ridiculous for blurting this out without thinking that she laughed. But Kitahara-san didn't seem to hear.

"So you'll come then. You'll come," she said, almost flirtatiously, as if finally, *finally*, she'd managed to seduce someone into accepting one of her invitations.

It was Kyoko's cousin, Mitsu, who had first introduced Kitahara-san. Kyoko and Mitsu had gone to see a play in which a guy from the food company where Mitsu worked before she got married had a very small role. Her cousin's main objective was to pursue the guy

(even though she was married now), and all Kyoko was really interested in was the dinner they planned to have afterwards. So when
a woman friend of some mutual acquaintance accosted them in the
foyer after the performance, Mitsu did her best to keep the conversation as short as possible, and Kyoko simply nodded politely. The
woman was Kitahara-san. In ocher-colored vest, white tunic, and
purple flared skirt embroidered in yellow at the hem, her outfit was
strangely folkloric. Long, shiny brown hair, and narrow, red-framed
glasses completed the look.

At first glance she seemed to be in her late twenties or early thirties, but on closer inspection it was difficult to tell. She could easily be an older person who looked young for her age. But judging
from the way she and Mitsu spoke to each other, they appeared to
be roughly the same age. Mitsu was thirty, two years older than
Kyoko.

They stood there listening to Kitahara-san go on and on end-
lessly about this mutual acquaintance of theirs. Finally, after glancing around and realizing there was no one left in the foyer except the
theater staff, Kitahara-san hesitatingly asked Mitsu what her plans
were for the rest of the evening.

Mitsu shot Kyoko a glance and said, "Um . . . tonight I've arranged
to have dinner with my cousin."

Kitahara-san immediately turned toward Kyoko as if to check her
reaction, but from behind her glasses came a pleading look, which
hit Kyoko with full force.

"But . . . uh . . . you're welcome to join us!" said Kyoko, quick to take the hint. This was the girl whose grade school report card used to say, *Always tries to please.*

"Really?" Kitahara-san's face broke into a radiant smile.

"Are you sure it's okay?" whispered Mitsu.

"Sure, it's fine," nodded Kyoko.

And that was how they ended up going to a curry restaurant near the theater with Kitahara-san. Once there, the first thing that became obvious was that Kitahara-san and Mitsu barely knew each other. And then, Kitahara-san—who didn't seem to like spicy food much and had ordered the mildest thing on the menu—kept making exaggerated gasping sounds every time she took a mouthful of curry. Her repeated cries of "Ooh, that's so hot!" while grimacing like a little girl or an old lady, killed any attempts at conversation. And as it was Kitahara-san who had kept the conversation afloat in the first place, the three of them were now reduced to sitting there making the odd desultory comment while her reproachful huffing and puffing echoed around the table.

At first, they managed to reply to every gasp with a polite "Really?" or "Spicy, isn't it?" or "I know!" but they soon ran out of things to say, and even the kindhearted Kyoko started to get fed up with repeating the same thing over and over again. Kyoko and Mitsu had planned this dinner some time ago; Kyoko had even written *curry* on her calendar at home, her sole engagement for that day. And now here was this woman spoiling their fun with her irritating complaints of "Hot! Hot!" It was enough to put you off your food.

No. That was mean.

Come on, Kyoko, she chided herself, making a renewed effort to help her cousin out with the job of sprinkling appropriate conversational gambits into any gaps that appeared between Kitahara-san's exclamations. That was when she found out that Kitahara-san was a passionate fan of a certain young theater troupe.

Kyoko herself knew nothing more about the troupe than their name, but she had a friend who had recently become crazy about them. As soon as she mentioned this, Kitahara-san erupted into a frenzy of excitement. "You *must* introduce me! I *have* to meet her!" she burst out, jet black eyes flashing through her glasses.

So, three days later, Kyoko found herself meeting up with Kitahara-san again, this time bringing along four old friends. She hadn't set things up especially for Kitahara-san; this happened to be an arrangement she and her friends had made a while back. Honestly, when she'd mentioned on the night of the curry that she was meeting these friends three days later, it was just to keep the conversation moving, but Kitahara-san had pounced immediately. "Three days from now? I'll come! I'll come!" Smiling delightedly from ear to ear, she had pulled a red diary, decorated with a bank logo, from her rattan handbag and started to make a note of the date.

"Cheers."

"Cheers."

"Cheers."

"Cheers."

For some reason, Kitahara-san's voice seemed to ring out the loudest. After the toast came a round of introductions. They'd met up in one of those Aussie Beef chain restaurants. Kyoko had asked her cousin if she wanted to come, just in case, but Mitsu had refused point-blank, saying she was busy. So Kyoko found herself with little to tell the others about Kitahara-san. For a start, she didn't even know how old she was. When she'd asked her, all she'd got in reply was, "Oh, we're about the same." She'd forgotten to ask what she did for a living, and when she'd checked with Mitsu she just got a plain "Dunno," so even if Mitsu had been there, it probably wouldn't have made that much difference.

On that day, Kitahara-san was wearing a figure-hugging, sky-blue, summer knit dress, a world away from the previous folkloric look. It wasn't a question of whether one style suited her more than the other; she was probably someone who had all kinds of looks. Kyoko sat Kitahara-san at the far end of the table with her friend Fuko, who liked the same theater troupe, so that the two of them could talk. Soon they were deep in conversation. The troupe's main appeal seemed to be the girlish good looks of the young male actors, but when Kitahara-san showed Kyoko the magazine clippings she'd brought along, Kyoko nearly spat out her beer. As far as Kyoko could see, there wasn't one good-looker amongst them. But despite their completely unremarkable faces, they were all desperately posing for the camera, doing their best to look cool.

Before long, Kyoko noticed that Kitahara-san was whipping out that familiar red business diary again, and pricked up her ears. She and Fuko seemed to be planning their next restaurant rendezvous. They were talking about going to a yakitori barbecue place that the young members of the theater troupe were rumored to frequent. These fanatics lived in a different world, thought Kyoko, allowing herself a gently mocking smile, as if to say that she couldn't *imagine* what the two of them were getting so excited about. Then suddenly Fuko called over, "Hey! You're coming too!"

No, no, it's impossible, I can't! she wanted to protest, but she couldn't get the words out; she was too nice for her own good. But she felt guilty about trying to dump this acquaintance of a cousin on one her own friends. Fuko had never even met Mitsu, after all.

That was how a reluctant Kyoko found herself on her third outing with Kitahara-san, this time to the yakitori restaurant supposedly patronized by a group of young actors she didn't even like. And this was barely ten days after their first meeting. But she knew that people could get pretty worked up when it came to the things they were passionate about, so she guessed she didn't really mind meeting her again so soon. Unfortunately, the young actors were nowhere to be seen. Undeterred, Kitahara-san was in relentlessly high spirits; tall glass of cassis and soda in one hand, chicken liver skewer in the other, shifting in her seat and craning her neck as her eyes swept the room. Now and then her pink lamé two-piece would sparkle brightly in the flash of the disposable camera with which she and Fuko were surreptitiously taking snaps of each other, as though this was a night to remember. It looked as though the two were well on the way to becoming firm friends, united by their common passion. But no sooner had Kyoko breathed a sigh of relief, than Kitahara-san's dear new friend Fuko—snatching a moment when Kitahara-san was in the bathroom—confessed that she really didn't like the woman; she just wasn't her type. Kyoko was crushed. The match had been a complete failure.

"Oh . . . I'm sorry," she apologized to Fuko. They quickly brought the evening to a close, taking care not to say anything that could possibly lead them into a next date with Kitahara-san, then went their separate ways.

And just when she was thinking that she wouldn't hear from Kitahara-san again, these phone calls had started to come. Kyoko knew she should have refused immediately if she didn't want to go. Instead, she acted all nice, and before she knew it, everything had become horribly complicated. It wasn't so much that she minded going to Kitahara-san's place; it was more that she felt uncomfortable being pursued like this.

But as soon as she had decided to tell her exactly what she thought, there was Kitahara-san with that syrupy voice of hers, purring, "Well, actually, I have a little favor to ask you," in artificially confidential tones.

I can't believe this is happening, thought Kyoko. She shuddered as she listened. It turned out that the favor she needed was some help with her computer settings. Kyoko could only think that Kitahara-san was taking a gamble on the fact that she had once mentioned she used to work in systems management when she was a secretary, and that she occasionally updated the home page for the florist's where she now worked part-time.

"Why me? Wouldn't it be better to ask a guy?" asked Kyoko, annoyed, pounding her fist on the green cover of the single bed where she sat. The more the two of them spoke on the phone, the better they were getting to know each other, although Kyoko had no desire for any such intimacy. "You don't have a boyfriend, do you? It'd be a good chance to ask someone you like."

"No boys allowed around here," Kitahara-san replied, in a coquettish voice.

This sucks, thought Kyoko. Here they were, two grown women, talking about boys as if they were schoolgirls. She gave a defeated sigh.

"Hey, you really should see a doctor, you know."

That was the advice of Kyoko's husband, whom she had divorced a year ago. But he was laughing when he said it, because it was still their honeymoon period. They were living in a cozy little condo over a home improvement center. He made the suggestion because although Kyoko was furious that the neighbor's cat had shit in the planters she had put out on the balcony, if ever she happened to meet the neighbor with the cat in his arms, she would always say, "Oh, it's such a cute little thing!" She wasn't just making polite conversation, nor was she being sarcastic. It wasn't some kind of curse she had looked up on the Internet either. At that moment she really did think the cat was cute, and she couldn't help saying so.

"Oh well, you'll just have to give up on the planters then. Because that's what cute little cats do, you know," said her husband, triumphantly, a staunch defender of the cat from the outset.

"No way," replied Kyoko. But she still found it hard to bear a grudge against the cat. The balcony, an extension of the roof of the home improvement center, had long been on the cat's circuit as it went for its daily prowl, and even before she had planted anything, she used to picture the grey-and-black striped tabby strolling around contentedly amongst her carefully cultivated herbs, trees, and flowers. With this gorgeous vision in mind, she happily poured leaf mulch into two long planters she had set out. But no sooner had she planted marigold seeds and eggplant seedlings, than the cat turned the planters into a toilet. The soil she'd prepared so carefully was now soaked in piss and littered with turds.

She couldn't simply turn her back on her long-cherished gardening dreams, but she hated the idea that the cat had obviously decided to make a toilet of the planters and do its business there every single day. She thought about taking preventative measures of some kind, but she didn't really know what effect they might have, and hesitated to try anything too strong for fear of upsetting the neighbor. In the end, both planters were left sitting empty in a corner of the balcony until the day she moved out.

"Come over any time . . . tomorrow . . . the day after . . . ," insisted Kitahara-san, completely ignoring any plans Kyoko might have had. This insistence wasn't because the computer thing was particularly urgent, Kyoko realized. It was just her personality. And maybe also because she was unemployed at the moment and had a lot of free time on her hands. Fuko, or someone, had asked what she did for a living, the second time they all met.

"Me? Oh, I'm recharging my batteries at the moment," Kitahara-san had replied, straight-faced.

"*Batteries?*" mocked Kumao, job-hopper and biggest slacker in the group. But Kitahara-san only laughed coolly in response, seeming neither embarrassed nor offended. Apparently, she used to work at a major trading company, although whether that was the truth or not was anybody's guess.

That Wednesday, her day off from the florist's, Kyoko had decided she would go to Kitahara-san's place in the afternoon. Armed with a map she'd had her fax over the night before, she pointed her parents' big silver sedan in the direction of the suburb where Kitahara-san lived. To go by train would have involved lots of changes and taken about an hour and a half, but it would probably take no more than thirty or forty minutes by car. Even allowing for midday traffic jams, she didn't anticipate any problems.

She pulled out the bunch of CDs that were stuffed into the storage compartment next to the handbrake. While waiting at the stoplight, she flicked through the titles, but there was nothing except classical, and old-fashioned Japanese ballads, so she opted for no music at all. She used to drive a lot when she was married, and she would sometimes run deliveries for the florist's, so she really wasn't such a bad driver. In fact, she was quite proud of her smooth, straight-line acceleration.

Since the divorce, Kyoko had been living with her parents. If she came home from work too tired to help around the house, her mother, a dedicated, full-time housewife, would give her a hard time. "You're so damn lazy! Why don't you take a leaf or two out of Kei's book, living out there in Sendagi with her mother-in-law?" It was true that Kei, a childhood friend, had been married for five years, and Kyoko knew that she was in no position to criticize when her own marriage had fallen apart after only a year and a half, but what was so great about five years if you were having an affair with a married man, as Kei was? Her mother didn't know that, of course. Her father, who had always spoiled his daughter, would occasionally pipe up, "You've always got a home here you know," as though he was reciting some cheesy line from a soap. Apart from that, he said nothing at all about Kyoko's divorce, certainly nothing critical.

Driving through a busy shopping district, she pulled into a parking lot next to the main road and bought some slices of cake from a pastry shop as a gift. Then she went to a nearby department store where she had an ice cream and a little rest. The roads had been busier than she expected and she was never going to make it there by two o'clock as promised, so she called Kitahara-san on her cell phone to say she'd probably be late. Even though she'd made it clear that Kitahara-san shouldn't bother cooking anything, the woman had apparently been preparing supper since morning, and her voice betrayed great excitement. "Don't be long now! Don't be long!" she urged.

Things started to cool off with her husband after they'd been married about ten months. So when it was time to make plans to celebrate their first wedding anniversary, things were already ice-cold. Despite this, it was her husband who—in a thoughtful gesture that was out of character for him—made the suggestion that they should do something to mark the occasion. Restaurant reservations were made, presents were bought, they got all dressed up, but just as they were stepping out of the door, he snorted, "What are you so excited about? This is stupid."

Had he deliberately set it up as a trap? Kyoko couldn't be sure. She had gone through a stage of wondering how someone who used to be so nice could have changed so much. But eventually she realized he probably hadn't changed. He was still the same person; it was just his feelings for her that had grown cold. She had known right from the start that he could sometimes say nasty things, but that side of him had gradually grown more pronounced, until finally he became the kind of person who never said anything nice.

If only she could say, "What did you say something like that for?" But she knew it was useless, so she kept her mouth shut. All she could think was, this was the person she had married.

"You've got a really vindictive streak, you know that?" he would say. "Even when you're totally pissed, you keep saying you're okay, there's nothing wrong, but you make sure you've got this look on your face that says you're not okay at all. It makes me sick."

Perhaps due to the strain of all the bad feeling between them, Kyoko had a mild attack of hyperventilation, crouching down on the kitchen floor with her hand over her mouth. He came close enough to hand her a white plastic shopping bag, and then stood there looking down at her as she held the bag to her mouth.

"You know, those empty planters on the balcony, if you're not going to use them, you should put them away. I don't know why you've left them out there. You hate that cat really, don't you? It destroyed your little dream. But no. All you can say is the cat is cute."

Kyoko wanted to throw the bag at her husband, but somehow she couldn't detach it from her mouth. It was only when he walked off that she was finally able to get the bag away from her face. But her breath still came in ragged gasps.

"I reckon it's time you went to the hospital for a checkup. I honestly think there's something wrong with you," he said, when she came out of the kitchen.

Kyoko clenched her hand into a fist and slowly started to raise it in the air so she could pound him on the head, without a word, as he sat on the sofa. In the end she just walked out of the front door without a word instead. There was no way a marriage like that was going to last.

Even without the GPS navigation system that every other car seemed to have these days, she managed to find the condo. When she called to ask where to park, Kitahara-san told her to wait, and quickly hung up. In a flash, she was running out of the glass-walled entrance hall and tripping down the front steps, a beaming smile on her face. Today she was dressed in an oversize purple T-shirt, and jeans.

"Kyoko!" Kitahara-san called out, still halfway down the steps, beckoning towards the car, where Kyoko was waiting with the window rolled down. Kitahara-san had suggested they call each other by their first names at their second meeting, but Kyoko had not yet managed to make the move to first-name familiarity. Following Kitahara-san's waved directions, Kyoko moved the car off the sidewalk in front of the condo where she'd parked, then pulled up tight against the wall of the building, so as not to block access to the parking lot. The condo was quite a nice low-rise design in beige, flanked on each side by luxury residences, whose trees and shrubs provided an attractive green backdrop.

"You're late!" gushed Kitahara-san, as though she'd been waiting for Kyoko to get out of the car so she could reprimand her. It was almost three o'clock. Kyoko apologized, gave her the cakes, and together they went inside the building. "Did you get lost or something?"

"No." Kyoko's brusque reply contrasted sharply with Kitahara-san's syrupy tones. Kyoko was surprised at her own curt manner.

"You're late," said Kitahara-san again, but quietly this time, as if to herself.

Her place was on the fifth floor. The door of the elevator slid open to reveal a narrow, windowless hallway, thick with silence. There appeared to be only one apartment at either end. Kitahara-san turned left, and Kyoko followed her down the hallway and through a dark blue door she had apparently left unlocked. The spacious entrance hall where Kyoko took off her sneakers was tiled in what looked like marble, and illuminated by three spotlights placed above the white, built-in shoe cabinet. A very low step marked the threshold between the entrance hall and the rest of the apartment.

"Great place you have," said Kyoko, impressed.

"Oh?" replied Kitahara-san smugly.

The apartment seemed quite large. When Kyoko asked how many rooms she had, Kitahara-san replied that there were three bedrooms, a living room, dining room and kitchen, and asked if she would like to see them all. Kyoko nodded. Kitahara-san went from room to room, switching on the lights as she went. First were two rather small Western-style rooms, then she showed her the bathroom and toilet.

"You do live alone, don't you?" Kyoko double-checked.

"Uh huh."

"How much is the rent?"

"Well . . ."

"You mean you bought it?"

"Yeah. But my parents put down half."

"Hey, you're not divorced, are you?"

"No! Not a chance. No way. I'm single. Still single," she insisted, repeating herself rather needlessly, thought Kyoko. But she decided to ignore the fact that Kitahara-san was getting all worked up again for no apparent reason.

"So you're a little rich girl, then."

"Oh no, far from it," she replied in the same smug tone as before.

"Wow," said Kyoko. She felt like a pauper child visiting a wealthy person's home for the first time. And while she was playing the pauper, she might as well continue her crude line of questioning. Had she paid off the mortgage? Kitahara-san nodded. Kyoko gasped in amazement again. Perhaps the story about recharging her batteries after working for a top trading company was true after all. And if that was the case, she couldn't be that young.

"And what's in here?" Kyoko called out as Kitahara-san seemingly deliberately walked straight past what must have been the last room, marked by a plain wooden door at the end of the wooden-floored hallway, just before the entrance to the living room. Kitahara-san swung around with split-second speed, her long brown hair flying all over the place.

"No! Don't open it!"

Kyoko felt shocked and a little embarrassed at Kitahara-san's unexpectedly harsh tone of voice. It wasn't as if she'd had her hand on the doorknob. And anyway, the woman said she could see all the rooms, didn't she? Maybe she'd had one of those big cleaning-up sessions, the way you do before people come over, and thrown all her junk in there. All the rooms she'd seen so far had been simply furnished and perfectly tidy. Well, whatever . . . She decided she wasn't really that interested, and let it drop.

In the huge living room was a sturdy, family-sized dining table, a TV, a video cabinet, and a wooden telephone stand that seemed to double as a storage cupboard. Why did she have such an enormous dining table? And why had she placed it at the furthest end of the room from the adjoining kitchen? All there was in the empty space in front of the kitchen was an immense Persian rug.

From the moment she walked through the front door, Kyoko had the distinct impression that hardly anyone ever came visiting here. She had thought maybe she felt that way because she herself wasn't that close to Kitahara-san, but now she was starting to realize that her first impression had been right. For one thing, there were only two chairs facing each other across the dark wooden table with the small lace cloth in the middle.

"Sit down, sit down," urged Kitahara-san sweetly, her recent harsh rejoinder apparently all forgotten. Kyoko sat down on the nearest chair. Kitahara-san disappeared into the kitchen, which Kyoko couldn't see from where she was sitting, and before long came back out again carrying a red mug and a blue mug. She placed the blue mug in front of Kyoko. It was a hot malted drink, the kind made by simply dissolving powder in milk. Her own special welcoming treat.

"I really thought you weren't coming, you know. You were so late!" Red mug beneath red-framed glasses, Kitahara-san sipped her drink slowly with narrowed eyes, relieved perhaps to have got this first task over and done with.

"Come on, give me a break," said Kyoko, with a small snort of exasperation. If she'd known Kitahara-san was going to be like this, she would have got there on time and left again immediately . . . Uh-oh. She was having mean thoughts again. "I did call to let you know I'd be late."

"Yes, but if you say you're coming to a friend's house at two, then it's only good manners to get there by two-fifteen. Don't you know that?" She withdrew her lips from the mug and spoke haughtily, like a teacher from a cheap finishing school. But her eyes were still narrowed, so she might have been smiling. "I've been cooking since this morning, you know. For dinner."

"Oh." Kyoko gave a noncommittal nod and drank her malted milk. "I did say that you shouldn't bother making anything, didn't I? I mean, you told me you never cook, right?"

"Yes, but when one's friends visit it's always nice to serve a home-made meal," she pronounced, lapsing back into schoolteacher mode. "And I'm sure you're going to like what I've made for you."

"Ooh. What is it?"

"It's a secret. You'll have to wait till evening," replied Kitahara-san excitedly.

"Oh . . . right," said Kyoko.

After she had sat there sipping her welcome drink for a suitably polite length of time, Kyoko thought it would be a good idea to get the computer problem out of the way. She'd do what she could, and what she couldn't do she couldn't, she stated frankly (even though it was obvious) as they headed to the room nearest the front door, which contained a computer, a table, and a bookcase. Whether dealing with Kitahara-san over the phone or face-to-face, Kyoko could always feel herself erecting this brusque facade to protect herself from the sweet stickiness emanating from the woman.

"I switched to broadband, and now I just don't seem to be able to connect to the Internet any more. It used to be fine." Before Kitahara-san had even finished opening the once briefly fashionable shell-shaped laptop, Kyoko had worked out what was wrong: the modem was switched off. Kitahara-san had apparently never bothered to check the little flat box lying there next to the computer. Kyoko almost couldn't believe it. But it was true.

"Must have done it on purpose," she muttered. But as soon as she said it, she felt bad because it sounded exactly like something her ex-husband would say. So she said, "Hey, great, we fixed it!" And Kitahara-san, delighted to have the problem solved, gave a great big smile, like an innocent child.

Dinner was rice topped with chicken and egg, and miso soup with clams. Kyoko ate while staring at the white feather fan from Juliana's Disco displayed behind the glass doors of the video cabinet, wondering how it could have taken so long to prepare such a simple meal.

They did rock-paper-scissors to choose from the cakes that Kyoko had brought, and washed them down with yet more malted milk.

"This is fun, right?" Kitahara-san nodded vehemently as she spoke, as if to confirm that this was most definitely the case. Kyoko forced a smile, but this didn't satisfy Kitahara-san.

"It's fun, isn't it?" she persisted.

"Hey, don't you think this is fun?" she tried again.

"Isn't this fun? . . ."

After being asked for about the fourth time, Kyoko felt obliged to nod in agreement.

"So you'll come again, won't you?" She got to her feet and trotted off down the hallway, returning with her red business diary. It was the first time the diary had been opened right in front of Kyoko; her first chance to take a peek inside. She had imagined the pages would be crammed full of appointments to meet this friend and that friend, but of course they weren't. Just the usual kinds of reminders were written here and there.

"When shall we say?" asked Kitahara-san, the tiny pen from the spine of the diary poised, a pleading look in her eyes.

"I'm not coming again." This time, Kyoko didn't mince her words. Kitahara-san laughed ever so sweetly, as if she thought Kyoko was teasing her. Or perhaps she was embarrassed. But she snapped the diary shut, for the time being at least.

They watched a short music video and laughed at the fashions in an old magazine. But when Kyoko went to the bathroom, she happened to notice that her sneakers had disappeared from the entrance hall where she had left them. For a brief instant the hairs stood up on the back of her neck, but when she went back into the living room and asked Kitahara-san where her shoes were, Kitahara-san, in a quiet voice, reassured her that she'd just put them in the shoe cabinet.

"Well, if you don't hand them over . . . ," she felt obliged to warn, deciding that the best way to counter such a childish prank was to mount an equally childish offensive, ". . . I'll open the door to that room!" She pointed toward the door that she had been warned so sternly not to open. Kitahara-san briefly stared in that direction, with an abstracted air, then threw a quick look at Kyoko.

"Open it if you want," she said, after a pause, in an awfully nice voice. Her face seemed suddenly to have aged. But now that Kyoko had permission to open the door, she couldn't really be bothered. She went back to the table, where Kitahara-san had got out her collection of black-and-white childhood snapshots for Kyoko's entertainment.

"If I ever get married, he's got to be good-looking. That's the way to have cute kids, isn't it?" She was prattling on like a little girl again.

"Sure."

"Don't you think?"

"Yeah. I guess you're right."

When nine o'clock came, Kyoko announced she was leaving, but it was ten by the time she managed to extricate herself. As they went down the hallway, Kitahara-san opened the door of the room

146

Inside

without being asked. "Here. Look." It was just an ordinary bedroom. It wasn't full of junk or garbage. There was only a bed covered with a simple bedspread. She didn't switch on the light and Kyoko didn't really get a good look, but in the faint glow cast by the light from the hall, it could have been a double bed pushed right up against the wall, or it could have been a single bed set slightly apart.

First published, 2004
Translation by Cathy Layne

Chiya Fujino was born in 1962. Her debut novel, *Afternoon Timetable*, was published in 1995, the first in a string of prizewinners. Fujino is a transsexual, but her stories do not particularly focus on gay or gender issues. Instead, she prefers to portray characters who are slightly out of step with society, and to hint at what may lurk behind the ordinary facade of everyday life. In 2000 she won the Akutagawa Prize for *Summer's Promise*, the tale of a group of friends in their twenties, centered around a gay couple and the transsexual next door.

Fiesta

Amy Yamada

*D*esire! There goes my mistress again, summoning me on a whim and getting me all flustered. It's always so unexpected. She hardly ever allows me the pleasure of unhurriedly putting together an outfit from the many clothes hanging in the closet. I suppose I'll just have to wear something simple in the same color as always. Oh, how I'd love to dress in sophisticated, subtle colors just once in a while! Never mind—I'm ready to go now. As you can see, this person who summons me treats me *terribly* well, as if she had never given so much as a thought to my hidden agenda. When I'm off duty, she plays me down to people on the outside. Sometimes it's as if I didn't even exist. *Just look at her, acting as though everything's fine*, I think to myself. Whenever such hateful thoughts rise up in me, I break through the thin skin beneath which I am so carefully concealed and expose a leg or something, as if by mistake.

Ladies and gentlemen, gather round and take a look at how ugly my mistress is! Every time I see her face reflected in the mirror, I feel deeply ashamed. Not only am I ashamed of the features of this face that covers me, but I am also ashamed of its resignation to its appearance, its anger, and—worst of all—its vain hope, all of which have meshed into a fine veil of unattractiveness that floats around her. I have to let out a sigh.

There is no such thing in this world as an ugly woman who is pure and innocent. If such a person exists, I'd be really grateful if you would let me know. And is an ugly woman really so different from a beautiful woman, anyway? Romeo would still have fallen in love with Juliet if she'd kept her mask on at the ball, right? Perhaps what ugly women need to realize is that life is a masquerade, and as long as they wear their masks forever, they will be making the most of their ugliness. Besides, true beauty is nothing but an illusion. On any given day, we must meet, what, five new people? Ten? Fifteen? It's always easy to overturn the standards of beauty, depending on who's around us. I can assure you that the course of history wouldn't have changed a bit whether Cleopatra's nose had been an inch longer or an inch shorter. And you know why? Because I refuse to work myself into the ground for the sake of an inch. Who gives a damn about an inch?

I can't remember how many years it's been since my mistress started calling on me for the sake of a certain specific Man. Sometimes she calls me when the Man is actually right in front of her, and sometimes when she merely conjures up an image of him. Either way, I'm being made to work toward the same goal. If I succeed, I'll be given the boot, exterminated, and although that will make me a little sad, I'll also be able to start looking forward to my reincarnation. Come on, Mistress! Isn't it about time you let me be reborn?

Obsession is by no means the birthright of ugly women. Beautiful women have their obsessions too. When the attention a woman pays to the object of her affections goes unreciprocated, Obsession is born, regardless of whether the woman is beautiful or ugly. The difference lies in the way beautiful women and ugly women deal with their Obsession. A beautiful woman sees Obsession clearly as a terrible, hideous brute who throws her into turmoil and jeopardizes her position. She is captive to this brute and begins to lose herself. *This wasn't supposed to happen*, she thinks. Obsession is a monster who thrives on her agony and ecstasy. But she shelters the monster carefully and does her best not to let him get out of hand.

For an ugly woman, Obsession is a different beast altogether. An ugly woman's first mistake is to afford her Obsession an undeserved status. It's really quite pitiful. As if that wasn't bad enough, then she summons me, Desire! I suppose she figures I'll lighten her load, but with Desire on hand, Obsession spins way out of control. You can see her bathing her Obsession over and over again, desperately trying to turn the monster into something beautiful, something completely new, with no impurities. Don't get me wrong—I'm certainly not jealous of his stylish new look. I mean, you can dress Obsession up all you like, but he's still nothing more than a hermit crab carrying the ugly woman on his back. The further the hermit crab walks, bearing his burden, the further removed Obsession becomes from his original monstrous form. Soon enough,

Obsession has risen from the muddy water he once loved so dearly and become a beautiful lotus flower. In a meadow named Pure Love in Full Bloom. The petals are whispering. *Murmur, murmur . . . murmur, murmur, murmur . . .* I listen closely, and I am dumbstruck. Against their better judgment, the petals are chanting in unison:

> *We'll always protect your simple heart.*
> *We'll never disturb your secret love.*

It makes my head ache. What's the point of working myself into the ground, when this is what I'm up against? Sure, it's all very easy when she's getting excited over a plate of food. All I have to do then is change into my gym clothes and hurry off to her aid. But this is something else. I'm telling you, there is nothing that exhausts me more than this kind of love, which my mistress mistakenly believes to be so pure. There's just no end to it, you know?

So here I am, grumbling about all of this, when suddenly I'm summoned again. My mistress's eyes are burning. I suppose I'd better go and help her out. As I set off, her eyes are already like magnifying glasses, enlarging the Man's image. He is facing his desk, concentrating on his work, and seems to be completely unaware of my mistress or anything else. His cold demeanor makes her mouth water. *Look at me*, she pleads silently, but of course he won't look. The Man is not aware of her feelings; he's not even conscious of her as a woman. She brings him a cup of coffee. *Thanks*, he mutters, without raising his head. She stares at him for just slightly too long. Meanwhile, I'm working like crazy. I maneuver the magnifying glasses, gathering up as much heat as I can and focusing it on a single point on the Man's body. The Man senses something and strokes the back of his head. She lets out a sigh—just a small one, so that no one notices—and walks away. My concentration breaks in a flash, and I am just about ready to collapse, but this is only the beginning. Now I am forced to enter into her reveries. It's always a difficult moment. I wonder how long I'll be held captive this time. *He loves me, he loves me not, he loves me . . .* On and on she'll go. Just the thought of it makes me exhausted. Hopefully one of her bosses will give her a chore and destroy the whole fantasy.

I don't mind that you don't notice me. I'll always watch over you because that's the nature of my love. I don't want anything from you. After all, true love is unconditional. I know you're seeing the Stupid Bitch from the Next Section, and I feel so sorry for you. You don't know that she's sleeping with our section chief, do you? She fucked that guy Suzuki too. And you know where? Yes, in the toilet of the bar we went to after the New Year party. When I think that you're being taken in by that tramp, I just want to protect you more and more. I'm not a vulgar woman. All I want is to love you with devotion. I truly believe that one day you will come to understand my feelings.

This is basically how my mistress's fantasy is structured. Excuse me, Mistress, but just how many years have you been *truly believing* all this? And to think I've been wasting my precious time on this Man for so long . . . I'm so jealous of the desires that live inside the Stupid Bitch from the Next Section. I bet they get to release themselves whenever they want, and don't have to sit festering like me. There's something wrong with this world. It's so unfair! Is this what happens to those of us born in an ugly woman's house? Do we have to go through life forever burdened with our pent-up emotions? Will origin always govern the fate of Desire? It's not that my expectations are too high. It's just that sometimes I feel so restless, and I need to shake it off. Not by eating, not by sleeping, and certainly not by shopping. If I were still a little kid, maybe doing some sport would help, but at my age? You've got to be kidding. Oh, this restlessness . . .

Actually, your whole identity is based on that restlessness.

What? Who is it spouting that bullshit? Oh, not you again, Reason. You think you're so damned clever, don't you? If you must know, while I sit here restless, all the time I'm gaining strength, so don't come around here with your wiseass words about identity. Everyone is bandying that word about recently, trying to bring me down, but I'm damned if I'm going to let them. You ought to have a little more respect. Let me tell you, I was ruling the world before humans became humans. It's just that now I've fallen on hard times, come under the control of my mistress, and here I am lighting fires with a magnifying glass. Or am I just making excuses for my fallen glory? What a depressing thought . . . Well, there's no time for that. A little more Pride, that's what I need. Pride? Hah! Pride, schmide. Pride is my worst enemy.

Let's move on to Passion. When we're in the grips of Passion, we're not simply thinking of the other person; we are consumed with a vision of them. I guess no one sees Passion as a negative thing, for Passion runs around dishing out Get Out of Jail Free cards to Self-Serving Love. Just the thought of Passion fills some people with longing, while others close their eyes and remember fireworks long ago extinguished. Those extinguished fireworks are the graves of their desires. It is a fact that folk who enjoy watching summer fireworks while sitting on tombstones generally take pleasure in their passions. I expect my mistress also cherishes her suffering as it smolders like a firework, and she probably doesn't feel guilty about doing so. No doubt she isn't even embarrassed that Passion is synonymous with Fanaticism. I bet she won't remember me so fondly when I'm dead and gone.

But what can I do? I'm nothing compared to her Passion, and that's why she treats me so badly. I dress in neat and tidy clothes that don't suit me and do my best to pretend to be pure and innocent. *But I am Desire, the King of Debauchery, and I will not rest until I have run the gamut of dissipation!* I'd love to be outrageous and shout something like that out loud, but I would never get away with it. Instead I have to act like a fine, upstanding young man. Fucking Passion. What's so great about Passion anyway? Passion just allows people to avoid reality. And my mistress's reality is that the Man won't even give her the time of day. What's worse is that she has Pride in there giving her a helping hand, providing her with the excuse that she and the Stupid Bitch are different. So why does she keep on summoning me? There must be some reason. Tell me, goddammit, tell me! If you don't tell me, there is nothing I can do. If you want me to stage an uprising for you, I am ready and willing!

Anyway, my mistress returns to her desk so overcome with Fanaticism (sorry, *Passion*) that she can't concentrate on her work for a while. The day appears to be passing by without a hitch, but I know for sure that all kinds of desires are whirling around the office. My mistress has stopped staring at the Man, but now that she's not actually looking at him, his image burns itself even more clearly into the back of her mind.

As I watch, it occurs to me that when love is unrequited, the flesh and blood of the human body become nothing more than information. It's surprising the extent to which this information has the power to consume a person's time. Now I am feeding on the Man's image, obtained through the eyes of my mistress. I gain strength from his body shape and his gestures. I can feel myself growing. She forms an image of his hand and gets Imagination to paint it into her picture of him. As I look on, the blurred picture gradually comes into focus. The hand Imagination has drawn is much more beautiful than the real thing, which of course works to my advantage. Before long, it begins to move. At this point, she stops wondering merely how it would feel to be touched by the hand, and instead begins to desire its touch.

Now is the time for me to pounce. I add substance to her depiction, whispering over and over: *You want to be touched, don't you? I know you want to be touched.* This is how I brainwash her. Needless to say, my mistress does not stand up and walk over to the Man to be touched; instead she just stays where she is, resisting her impulses. I have no release, so I run all around her body, but I can't find an exit. Ah, this is agony! Before long, her lower body starts to heat up. I am suffering in the heat, and I have to change my outfit again. My mistress tries to ignore it, but the heat is making her eyes glisten and her cheeks blush. What was that you called it? Pure Love? Ha! You don't fool me. I changed into Lust's clothes a long, long time ago.

You see, those who call Lust by Passion's name are too ignorant to know any better. My mistress is so lacking in self-awareness that she doesn't even know when she's in heat; and so it is Platonic Love that comes into play, while I remain ignored, even though I am forced to undertake this backbreaking work. Just who was it that labeled me *dirty*, anyway? Some humans have a palpable sense that their time of ignorant innocence has passed. I'm so envious of the desires dwelling in those people. What did I do to get stuck with this virtuous, ugly mistress? The passage of time means nothing to women like her. Well, I suppose it's better than lodging with an ugly woman who throws her Desire around indiscriminately, in defiance of her ugliness. I've heard it said that under those working conditions, my fellow desires are all sent to early graves, and that Reason doesn't even make it beyond the womb. So I suppose I should be grateful for what I have.

Well, would you look at that.

All of a sudden, Imagination has awakened her lips. *A kiss is an overture to love*, she thinks. *It wraps you up softly, and then glides away like a butterfly. A butterfly kiss.* And there Imagination hits a wall. Heh heh heh. To tell the truth, my mistress hasn't tasted a kiss since

Ishihara kissed her in the gymnasium storeroom in middle school, and even that was just one of those rare moments when the curiosity of two people happens to coincide. My mistress mistook that kiss for some sort of official stamp on her first love, but I know that Ishihara rinsed out his mouth at the water fountain in the schoolyard afterwards. She must have seen him too, but she pretends to have forgotten. He never visited the scene of the crime again. As for my mistress, well, she has lived her life to this day desperately trying to convince herself that a kiss signals the culmination of young romance. And that's why she doesn't know. She doesn't know that a kiss is a wet thing. Not the pinnacle of romance, but a warm-up to sex. *Right! Stretch your arms, bend your knees, good! Now, stretch your tongue, entwine with your partner, and dive in!* She doesn't know that a kiss is a way to generate heat.

Basically, my mistress ignores all bodily fluids except sweat. The thick, slimy, gooey bodily fluid engendered by a kiss is outside her experience, which means that I never get a chance to diffuse myself through her lower half. When it's summer, and the Man comes back to the office from his rounds, she considers the sweat on his brow to be somehow hygienic. The very same salty water may be dripping from his armpits, releasing a beastlike odor, but I don't bother to alert her attention to this. It appears that saliva, urine, and semen do not fall under the jurisdiction of Passion. If only she would summon me into the realm of these bodily fluids! Then I could show her just how debauched Desire can be . . .

With my mistress being the way she is, I just can't seem to

motivate myself when she wants be kissed or embraced, and I end up slacking on the job. When Desire cuts corners, the lower half of the body never becomes moist. Where's the fun in a dry kiss? Damn it, Mistress, will you please give me something to do? I was born as Desire after all, so I'd like to have the chance to live up to my name at least once before I grow old. I'm not saying you have to become a nymphomaniac or anything—I just wish you'd make use of your Tactile Senses a little more. I'm so tired of sacrificing myself for your empty daydreams. Tactile Senses are my masseurs. They're moaning about having nothing to do, too. *We're not just here for the fun of it,* they say. *We feel like bored geisha waiting around for customers.* Or words to that effect . . .

The funny thing about women like my mistress is that up to a certain age they consider their virginity as something to be gotten rid of, but after a certain age, they start to think it is something to be protected. But Mistress, what's the point of protecting your virginity when nobody wants to take it from you anyway? You waste all your thoughts on this Man, even though he won't give you a second glance, so why don't you just close your eyes to the obstacles that stand in your way and go get him? Just do it and see what happens. Go on, just do it! Oh, wait a minute, it's the Man who is closing his eyes . . . Well, that's no problem . . . makes it all the easier for us.

You know, I really don't think you should be pandering to these modern tendencies.

Yeah, yeah, there's Reason putting on his hesitant face again, but just forget about him. You'll never be happy if you try to go along with every little thing other people say. Whose life is it anyway? You have to go it alone in this world if you want to succeed. There's a long road behind me, littered with the cast-off shells of my previous incarnations. But now I'm stuck at a dead end . . .

So, here I am slacking off on lip work, and now she's started on her arms. *I want to be embraced*, she says. Oh you do, do you? You know, your lack of initiative really drives me crazy. Why *I want to be embraced*? Why not *I want to embrace him*? Your arms are long enough, and your shoulder bones are strong. In fact, there's nothing at all stopping you from embracing him. Give it a shot. Wrap that cold fish in your arms until your bones are about to break. Don't pay any attention to that snapping sound—there's an orthopedic clinic next to the office, remember? Having your arms in plaster as a result of embracing a man, now isn't that the height of luxury? And if you don't like that idea, just put a little more milk in your coffee for extra calcium.

Oops. Mustn't get carried away. I'm not supposed to be so considerate. I am Desire, after all.

A hug and a kiss. My mistress thinks that's all there is to it, but what would she hear if she were to lean in close to her body and listen? No doubt she would hear various voices raised in anger, and the loudest of those voices would be mine. More and more of the others are coming around to my way of thinking. A youthful leader—that's the role I've been given. It's a big responsibility, but I have to say it feels pretty good to have my very own followers. *The fear and the ecstasy of being the chosen one.* Now I understand what that means. This is Desire they're talking about here. Well, if that's the case, allow me to blow my own trumpet a little more. Who do you think ensures the survival of the human race itself? Yes, it is I, Desire. You really should take better care of me, you know. On TV in the olden days, children were born of hands clasped together on top of bedsheets, but times have changed. So start using your body's curves and contours! Or more to the point, let *me* use them!

So I'm standing here on my pedestal, enjoying my little ego trip, when all of a sudden I'm given the boot. I am about to protest, but then I realize why. Out of nowhere, the Stupid Bitch from the Next Section (© Mistress) has sidled up to the Man. I don't know what she's doing there, but there they are, huddled together over the computer screen. Anger calls out to me, all of a fluster: *I've just been called out on an external assignment! I think it's pretty urgent. See you later!* And off he runs. Jealousy is right behind him. *Wait! Don't leave me behind*, he shouts.

What is it with that bitch? She's so vulgar it makes me sick! Does she think she's beautiful or something? All she's doing is camouflaging herself in makeup, hiding the wrinkles on her face with three layers of concealer. Any woman can see that. Why are men so easily fooled by appearances? What an ugly fucking whore. But I will never be like that. I will love only you. Forever and ever. I don't mind standing on the sidelines. I'll never stop thinking of you with all my body and soul.

Objection! Liar! When have you ever used *all your body*? All you've ever used is your eyes. You do nothing but watch.

Well, I guess there are worse ways of going about it. She assumes complete control of the images of the Man that fly in through the open windows of her eyes. She uses these images to ignite the flames of love in her own private power generator. Unrequited Love is happy to hang around forever, so maybe there's no need for anything more. This must be how an ugly woman in love plays her cards. And maybe my role in the game is just to sit here smoldering away. If so, then she's not as dumb as she looks. All this time, I've been trying to get her to step up the pace, but perhaps she's perfectly content as she is.

The Stupid Bitch looks over and laughs. Maybe she sensed my mistress's stare. *Oh, I've got a good idea! Why don't we invite her to the party tonight?* she says, placing her hand on the Man's shoulder. The Man looks somewhat bemused, but he agrees. So the Stupid Bitch is planning to use my mistress as her foil, is she? I look around the office and see that everyone else knows it. Oh, now that pisses me off! Yeah, okay, okay, I know I ridicule her day in day out, calling her ugly and what have you, but this is something else. I'm consumed with rage. I urge my mistress to go tell her what she can do with her fucking invitation, but my mistress, being my mistress, just says *Thank you, I'd be delighted to join you.* There's no hope for her.

Then, just as I'm sitting there crying over my misfortune, Anger comes running up to me again, not quite so full of himself this time. *I don't think I can do it on my own. Can you help me, please?* Oh well, if I must. As I look through my clothes, thinking about what I should wear this time, I hear my mistress whispering to herself.

I want to kill that fucking bitch. I swear I want to kill her.

Whoa, hold on there, I think, but just in case, I put on my black suit. Maybe I'm jumping the gun a little. After all, no one is dead yet.

Silly me. I can't say I'm particularly delighted about working for Murderous Intent, but I guess I don't really have a choice in the matter. Anyway, this is just one more of her ambitions that will never reach fulfillment. Funnily enough, it's thanks to all those unfulfilled dreams that I've been able to seize the reins of power inside this woman and strut around as if I own the place. The pain of being unable to relieve myself has allowed me to climb to these heights. Isn't it ironic?

Long ago, we desires were humble entities, forced to conceal our very existence. I guess desires who remember those days would say we are living through better times now. Well, it's true that nowadays it is easier for us to find release, and in that respect, life has become more comfortable, but whether or not we are valued more is hard to say. As I sit here gritting my teeth, I can feel myself growing in intensity. It's as if I am learning the ways of my ancestors inside this utterly old-fashioned body, adopting the pose of a Desire who feigns humility, but in truth holds the key to his mistress's fate. A great, unexercised power sleeps in my breast. Nourished by the soul, it is waiting for the day it will be awakened.

I want to kill her! Ahh I want to kill her I want to kill her ohh I want to kill her . . . I sing my mistress's words back to her in the style of a Buddhist chant, but I adapt the lyrics so that she hears, *I want to be embraced! Ahh I want to be embraced I want to be embraced ohh I want to be embraced.* This is a little idea I developed all by myself to pass the time. It's pretty damn effective, even if I do say so myself. I got Reason in on it too, singing harmonies on the side. He's always whining about overtime compensation, but I haven't paid him a penny yet. Anyway, you scratch my back, I'll scratch yours—that's what it's all about, right? There, she seems a bit calmer now. I can take a break for a few minutes.

If you want to use me as your foil, go right ahead, but you might just regret it later. You may be reeling him in with your body now, but I'm the one who truly loves him. You and your body are just temporary diversions, like a bout of the flu. He understands the inner beauty of a woman. He appreciates the value of a woman who will love him selflessly. Yes, I'll go to the party tonight, and yes, I'll accept my role as your foil, but what if he just so happened to be moved by my purity? What would you do then?

Oh, she's so old-fashioned. She's so old-fashioned she has scarcity value. She could actually be worth quite a lot of money. I've tried so hard to love my mistress over the years, but now I'm starting to become vexed. I need to take a nap.

You're going to sleep now? That's not fair! Why don't you try thinking about someone other than yourself for a change? I ignore Reason's gripes and settle down to sleep. *Can't you just get her started on the Man again? I want a break too!* I can hear his voice going on and on, but I continue to ignore him. I guess it must be hard for Reason, having to hang out with me all the time, but it's his fault that I don't get to release myself. Of course, when I point this out to him, he looks all hurt and says that he doesn't do it on purpose. I suppose he's just doing his job.

When I am summoned from my deep sleep, the party is already beginning to heat up. I can't believe how quickly the time has passed. I must have been really tired. As I'm choosing an outfit, still half-asleep, Hatred runs up to me and urges me to hurry. Perhaps my mistress still wants to kill the Stupid Bitch, or maybe just beat her up this time. I put on my black suit again, just to be on the safe side, and rush to work. *It's all a bit of a disaster*, whispers Reason as we cross paths. *But I guess it means I can finally take a break.*

As I arrive, the Man and the Stupid Bitch are announcing their engagement. Everyone is giving them a big round of applause. Who would have thought? My mistress is clapping weakly. It's the first time I've seen Conditioned Reflex in action for a while. *Finally, a chance to show off my skills*, he says, all fired up, but soon his time is up, and he exits the stage reluctantly. The happy couple hold hands, their faces glowing with joy. Ah, the Man's hand. How many times has that hand touched my mistress in her world of make-believe? Before today, those touches still held promise.

I want to kill her. Ahh I want to kill her I want to kill her ohh I want to kill her. My mistress's face is deathly white, and her whole body is shaking. Yeah, that's it! Get even angrier! The Bitch only went for him because she knew he was the man of your dreams. Well, she's put an end to all that, so what do you have to lose? Remember what I called my mistress just now? Old-fashioned. For such old-fashioned women, the marriage of a man signifies the end of a dream. Most old-fashioned women are gracious in defeat, but not my mistress. In an instant, her love turns to hate, and this time I don't slack on the job. I sing at the top of my lungs. *I want to kill him! Ahh I want to kill him I want to kill him ohh I want to kill him.* She hates the

Man even more than the Stupid Bitch now. Again she stares at him, but this time her gaze is defiant, and more piercing than ever. Is there any greater proof of being crazy about someone than wanting to kill them? I am deeply moved. My ugly mistress is becoming more beautiful by the minute. She summons me and I go to her. From the bottom of my heart, and with every fiber of my being, I will do my utmost to serve her. I am staggered by the intensity of these feelings.

The Man stands up to go to the bathroom, feeling good in his drunkenness. Nobody sees him go. The engagement party becomes wilder as the alcohol flows, and soon no one even remembers what they are celebrating. The Stupid Bitch works her way around the table, pouring drinks for the other men and flirting with them one last time before she becomes a respectable woman. My mistress can't bear to listen to her, so she stands up and follows the Man. The Man is walking out of the bathroom, looking refreshed, but she pushes him back inside. *She wants to kill him,* I think. *Ahh she wants to kill him she wants to kill him ohh she wants to kill him.* But instead of killing him, my mistress chooses to rape him.

This time the one who hesitates is me. *Wait a minute! I'm in my best black suit here!* On second thought, I figure that even in mourning attire, Lust can be pretty attractive. *Yeah! Do it! Go on, do it!* Suddenly I realize that the voice that drives a person to have sex is the same voice that drives her to commit murder. Who would've guessed? Ah, who gives a shit? Okay, Mistress, now's your chance to do all those things you've always longed to do. You wanted to be touched, right? And you wanted to be kissed. You wanted to be embraced. Decency was holding you back, but I won't. Murderous Intent has torn the mask from Pure Love's face. So touch the bastard! Kiss him! Embrace him!

My mistress ignores the Man's protests and embraces him so hard I can hear his bones cracking. *Come on! You can do better than that!* I cry in excitement. She prizes his mouth open and inserts her tongue. *That's it, that's it! Give him a taste of that prime meat!* I am so filled with pleasure that I am about to lose control. I take a deep breath and watch closely. At last I have found release. I am being unleashed in a way I have never experienced. She unzips his pants and draws out what lies beneath. And there it is, the Man's Desire. Captured. Enslaved. I feel an acute sense of superiority as I look at it. I've become a Desire that looks down on other desires. At last I've reached my goal. I think of all the things I've wanted to do for so long, and the first is to laugh out loud. Ah ha ha ha!

Hey, Reason, sleep deep, kid! This is my time to dance. Tonight is my own private Walpurgis Eve.

Murderous Intent looks up at me with respect in his eyes. Hatred is moved to tears. Jealousy raises his eyes to the heavens and gives thanks. Pure Love sheds her skin and embraces Hopelessness. It's a fiesta! A party! A carnival! And I'm the guest of honor.

My mistress has drawn out the Man's belt and is using it to tie his wrists together. I am in love with her strength. Now I see that ultimate pleasure is achieved only at the peak of endurance. My mouth is full of fine food that I could never have tasted had I lived in a beautiful woman. I realize that the more I chew, the closer I come to my extermination, but I guess that's all right. I am resigned to the beauty of my eternal demise, bathed in all the fluids that can possibly flow out of a body. Any time now, my current incarnation will face certain death. I brush a speck of dust off my jacket. So this is why I chose my black suit. I thank Unconsciousness, and celebrate my death dressed correctly for the occasion.

First published, 2001
Translation by Philip Price

Amy Yamada, born in 1959, is widely considered the pioneer of a new generation of Japanese women novelists noted for their frank, sexually explicit portrayals of women's lives. Her first novel, *Bedtime Eyes*, published in 1985, is the controversial story of the relationship between a black American soldier and a Japanese woman. Since then, Yamada has written more than a hundred novels, essay collections, and short story collections, and has won many major literary prizes. Her novels *Trash*, *Bedtime Eyes*, *Jesse*, and *The Piano Player's Fingers* have been translated into English.

The Unfertilized Egg

Junko Hasegawa

The sky hangs heavy, a sleepy mixture of light and dark, lilac and indigo. The orange rays of the early morning sun glare through the gaps in the clouds, stinging my eyes as if to punish me for staying out until dawn.

It's like a psychedelic movie or something.

Loud music rings in my ears and reverberates inside my hollow skull. Sunlight and shadow mingle on the back of my eyelids like the groups of gossiping girls and loudmouthed guys at last night's wild party, and I feel as though I'm still there. It's as if all the debris of the night has been kicked up into my face by pointy boots and sequined mules, and has stuck there like dirt that can never be washed away. At my age, I guess I shouldn't be staying out all night in the first place.

I'm wearing a short silver dress, and my rabbit-fur jacket is draped over my shoulders. My friend Rei, ten years my junior, walks beside me in a red leather coat and denim miniskirt. To tell the truth, for most of the night I just wanted to go home, or at least go some place

The Unfertilized Egg

else. The pounding beat of the music made me feel dizzy, tired, and way too old. Instead of dancing, I plastered myself to the mirrored wall for hours on end, like a piece of dried-up gum.

I looked wistfully at every guy that barged into me, wishing he would take me somewhere quiet where we could sit down and flirt a little. But then Rei got pissed off and said this was a girls' night out and we should be having fun together, so in the end I didn't pick anyone up. After the club closed, the two of us staggered drunkenly into an all-night fast-food place where we could hang out until the trains started running. The fluorescent lights were so bright you'd think they did it on purpose. I sat at the counter and ordered the breakfast set, while the sullen, buck-toothed waiter stole glances at my cleavage.

"Hey, do you remember that guy with the bleached hair who was chatting me up? That was so funny!" For some reason my hands are shaking so much I can't hold my chopsticks.

"Which guy?" asks Rei halfheartedly, scraping a piece of glitter from her eyelid with her fingernail. She looks fed up. "You can have mine if you want. I'm not hungry." She nudges her bowl over to me.

Rei gets off the train at Naka Meguro, and I carry on to Toritsu Daigaku. Home at last, thank God. The sky has already brightened to a cold white. It's garbage day, and gangs of crows are hanging out on the sidewalk like small-time hoods. Or maybe they're more like mourners at an early-morning funeral, with their keening and crying. Ashes to ashes, dust to dust, and all that. The clap of high heels echoes in the stairwell as I climb up to my apartment. The stairs feel extra steep this morning. It's the second time this week I've stayed out all night.

I tumble through the door, take off my boots, and stagger along the hallway. I clear a space on the bed among the makeup, purses, and paper bags. Finally I can get some sleep. Goodnight. I'm out cold on my first breath, and plunge helter-skelter to the depths of unconsciousness, until I'm nothing more than sediment on the floor of my brain. I'll lie sprawled here now all morning, false eyelashes stuck to my cheeks like insect legs, bald patches on my toenails where the blood blister-colored lacquer has chipped.

I dream I'm holding a white egg in my hand. I'm in the produce section of a supermarket. The egg has been passed to me from somebody's hand as though I am being entrusted with something precious. The hand is attached to a bulging, muscular arm with reddish-black skin, and although for some reason I can't see a face or a body, the arm appears to belong to a well-built man. The blood vessels running under his skin are thick and remind me vaguely of the veins of a leaf. Suddenly, I hear a stern voice telling me to hold the egg more carefully. Viscous droplets are oozing out of the egg and flowing through my fingers to form a puddle on the floor. I feel so guilty. All I did was tighten my grip a little, and now I've gone and broken it.

What the hell are you doing? cries the voice angrily.

"I didn't mean to," I reply.

Fragments of shell are everywhere, on my fingertips and even under my fingernails. The slimy white of the egg sticks coldly to my hand. The yolk has fallen onto the floor and splattered all over the toes of my mules. I don't know what to do. How could I do such a thing right in the middle of the store? I stand there, without moving, in front of the refrigeration cabinets in the chilled food section. Then I decide to hide the remains of the broken egg in the tub of water where they keep the tofu. Just as I thrust my hand into the tub, I wake up.

It's shortly after two in the afternoon. I peel my head off the sheet beneath me, which stinks of dried saliva. My hair is sticking up like someone who's just had the fright of her life, and the shoulder straps of my dress are all twisted. I guess I should have taken it off before I fell asleep. I hear the sound of paper rustling. No wonder I'm aching; I've been lying on a magazine all night. The smiling face of the pinup girl on the crumpled front cover has become a twisted grimace. She glares up at me accusingly, as if it were my fault that she didn't sleep properly either. Like I care. I throw the magazine on the floor, and then sit up, pulling the string of my thong out of my ass. Every time I move my head of wild, morning hair, motes of dust dance whispering and sparkling through the air and fall in a shower of golden sand. Eventually they settle, forming a carpet of gilded moss over the clothes scattered on the floor, over magazines lying there like dead birds with outspread wings, and over the open drawers of my wardrobe. Behold my trash heap of an apartment. This tiny square of space I call my own does nothing to assert its existence, but is simply there, like a gap between buildings that no one ever passes through, lined with moldy, black sewage pipes. Every day I wake up to the same filthy mess, and it never fails to disgust me.

While I wait for the bathtub to fill, I go to the kitchenette and open the fridge. Apple juice, an orange, butter, mustard, wasabi, and behind them a huge stainless steel bowl. I kick a pile of magazines out of the way and sit on the floor with the bowl on my knees. The white, jellylike mass in the bowl is tapioca and coconut milk. I got the recipe from a TV show about dieting. They said coconut milk speeds up the metabolism, so I went straight out to the supermarket and bought all the ingredients. I soon discovered that a large can of coconut milk, a cup of milk, half a cup of water, and a cup of tapioca makes an enormous amount, so that's all I've been eating for the last two or three days. I thrust a dessert spoon into the bowl and begin to shovel it down as though it were rice porridge. It tastes vaguely sweet, and is kind of formless and indistinct. Just like my youth.

As I stare at the white jelly, it begins to look sordid somehow, and suddenly I remember the dream I had right before I woke up; the one where I broke the egg.

"Well, that was definitely a sex dream," I say disgustedly, with a grain of tapioca stuck to my lip. I bet the younger girls in the office gossip about me: "Time's running out for Moriko. She's already in her thirties. Poor thing." Or: "She hasn't had sex for ten years, you know. She's practically a virgin again. She'll seal up if she doesn't get some soon."

I put the bowl down and stare into space. I'd love to tell those rude bitches that actually the last time someone ventured into my cave was only a month ago. But then, I guess there's really not much difference between one month and ten years. It's all too easy for a woman to fall apart when the dark frontier between her legs, her empty building, her spider's cave, is left unexplored even for just one night. Only women who are loved fully and warmly, right through to their bones, are complacent enough to say they can't be bothered with sex.

It's all that bastard Aono's fault. One night we stopped having sex after dates, and then he disappeared overseas on business. He still hasn't come back, and it's been over a month. So here I am, all frustrated, breaking eggs in my dreams and making masses of white, jellylike stuff.

I press my tongue against the roof of my mouth, where the faintly sweet aftertaste of coconut milk lingers. Aono would be amazed if he knew I lived in this squalor, sitting here naked except for my thong, with scraps of paper sticking to my bare ass, shoveling down tapioca and coconut milk. He'd never think for a minute that I live like some desperate teenage runaway. The young guys at work call me the "Legendary Dancing Queen." I guess they're only joking around. They probably see me as a kind of respectable older-sister type. But recently, my reign appears to be coming to an end. After all, what kind of queen stays out at clubs all night, eyeing cheap-looking guys but getting no response, much to the disgust of her younger friends? What kind of queen eats fast food at dawn, gets screamed at by crows on the way home, and collapses fully clothed into bed to sleep like the dead? And then has these thinly disguised sex dreams . . . I'm just a sad, sleazy slut.

But hold on a second. I have an excuse.

Yesterday was my thirty-sixth birthday. That pile of trash by the front door is actually a birthday present from Aono. It arrived last week by airmail: a crystal vase and a box of Godiva chocolates. Kind of like a Christmas present from someone who got the dates mixed up. And would you fucking believe it? There were thirty-six chocolate truffles in the box, all lined up, present and correct. I sent him an e-mail telling him not to make me thirty-six a week early, but the bastard didn't even send a reply. So it seems my Aono is incommunicado.

Marilyn Monroe was thirty-six when she met her mysterious death. Princess Diana was thirty-six when she died in a car accident just before she remarried, and the writer Izumi Suzuki was thirty-six when she committed suicide. Thirty-six is a woman's unlucky number, a bad omen. I bet the only reason Aono stopped having sex with me is because I was about to turn thirty-six.

Once, when my grandmother was still alive, I had a conversation with her and my mom about how all of us—three generations of women in the same family—were born in the Year of the Horse, and all shared the same blood type, B.

"Moriko, you make sure you have a little B-type girl in the Year of the Horse!"

"We've got to keep the record going!"

"Wouldn't it be wonderful?"

I was still in middle school at the time, and it wasn't really anything more than mindless chatter, but I'm sure the two mothers were only half-joking.

My grandmother passed away without ever seeing her wish fulfilled. I'm ashamed to say that at twenty-four I was quite happy to have sex with men, but I wasn't even close to getting married, let alone giving birth. So if I don't have a baby now, at thirty-six, my next chance is forty-eight, but by then my uterus won't be in any sort of working order, and my mom might not even be alive.

Mom, Grandma, I'm so sorry.

To tell the truth, all this stuff about giving birth to a girl with B-type blood in the Year of the Horse hadn't crossed my mind for years, but it all came back to me as soon as I realized I'd be turning thirty-six. A month ago, in a bar in Shinjuku, I told Aono about this chain of B-type, Year-of-the-Horse daughters. He seemed pretty interested. I remember him laughing as I told him. Maybe he thought I was making it up. But that was the night we stopped having sex. Then he went off on his overseas business trip, and I celebrated my birthday without him for the first time in the four years since we met.

On my birthday, I felt as though a timer had been set in the depths of my belly, in that place where my female functions writhe slipping and sliding with the wax and wane of the moon. Two months left, said the timer. No more than two months to get started on fulfilling my grandmother's dream. I could even hear the needle ticking away the time. The sound was unbearable. I figured that if only I could drown it out with some loud music, some noise and laughter, maybe even a drunken fight, then somehow I'd be able to get through the night of my thirty-sixth birthday.

I lower myself into the bathtub with a deep sigh. I touch my belly with the tip of my finger, and press lightly against the gentle resilience of flesh and fat. Slowly, I let my finger slide downward, and there, beneath the tuft of grass, lies my vulva, like a rafflesia flower thriving on the dark, damp ground of a remote South Pacific island. The world's biggest flower, with its grotesque, blubbery petals open to the gloom. In this dark wetland, surrounded by ferns, the petals of my rafflesia shimmer with sparkling pollen and laugh coquettishly.

You'd better hurry up and get yourself fertilized! There isn't much time, they say.

My God, I'm being goaded by my own vulva.

Well I can't just walk up to Aono and beg him to fertilize me— not my secret sugar daddy. His blood type is B too, by the way.

Aono and I are huddled together in a bar. I sit there sadly, turning my glass round and round. I watch the small waves of golden liquid ripple across the surface of my drink, while next to me Aono is acting like an excited child—stretching out the skin on his forehead and then squeezing it together with his hands, trying to show me how he can form the Chinese character for "flame" with his wrinkles. I look up at him irritably, and he takes my sunken cheeks in his hands. He lets out an affected sigh and whispers, "You have no cheeks, do you?" I puff out my cheeks in anger and tell him to stop pissing me off, at which point he bursts out laughing. "Now you have cheeks!" he says.

Although he's my boss, it's always me who's the bossy one when we're alone together. He's the perfect gentleman—immaculately dressed, faultless in every way. His wife was Miss Keio University, and his son is studying to be a doctor at another prestigious school. So what does he see in me, the office spinster, with her dirty dreams? Four years is too long for a fling, and he can't possibly still see me as some happy-go-lucky young girl, bouncing around all plump and juicy. Maybe he thinks I'm some dedicated career woman who doesn't believe in marriage. Aono doesn't know that my room is filthy, or that I sing in the bathtub. I've never smelled his bad breath or laughed at his morning hair when he wakes up. There are so many things I can't say to him, and so many questions I want to ask him but daren't.

One day, we were fooling around in GAP on Shibuya Koen Street. There was a hat on sale for about a thousand yen, and he was begging me to buy it for him. It was a woolly, green, pull-on hat, and obviously far too young for him. Besides, I'd never even seen him wear a hat for as long as I'd known him. He told me he wanted something he could tell people Moriko had bought for him.

"Quit fooling around," I scolded him, haughtily, but he seemed to enjoy being admonished. I cuffed him on the head and told him to wipe the silly grin off his face. As we walked on and on up the street, fooling around like kids, I felt I would go anywhere with him. I thought that if we could only keep walking straight ahead, never getting into a car, never turning a corner, we would come to a place where all our problems (well, my problems, I suppose) would be solved.

About twenty years ago, "first time" movies were all the rage. At one point, these bittersweet classics were being churned out in huge quantities, but they rarely make it onto DVD. Even if they do, they don't sell. I can remember them all: *The Blue Lagoon* with Brooke Shields, *Paradise* with Phoebe Cates, *La Boum* with Sophie Marceau . . . They pretty much all went the same way: the teenage heroine spots a cute young guy, their paths cross, they fall in love, they have sex for the first time, and then—as they finally reach the doorway to true love—the story ends. As an adult, these movies are almost painful to watch. You feel kind of sad, and at the same time slightly ashamed of yourself with your sagging ass in its sexy underwear. There were other movies that laid on the sex more thickly, like *Fast Times at Ridgemont High* and *Little Darlings*. Either way, they always ended with "the first time." I love those movies. When I was in middle school, I used to buy magazines like *Roadshow* or *Screen*, and just reading about these movies would feel somehow illicit. Remember *Paradise*, with the teenage boy and teenage girl alone in the desert? All very erotic, and totally unrealistic. And then there's the obligatory bathing scene, right? Where the girl always says, "Don't look!" Then, in the last scene, when the young lovers are doing it for the first time, they're in a fabulous meadow full of flowers, while in the background the *Paradise* theme song—sung by Phoebe—plays right through from beginning to end. Of course they never showed you the details. There were no undulating hips, and she didn't give him head or anything. Right up until I actually did it myself, I thought the guy just had to stick it in, and that was sex. They never make those first time movies anymore, do they? I wonder why.

"Nobody wants to watch movies like that," says Uchiki, a young guy from the office, dismissing my lengthy discourse on the subject. I work for a video import company whose policy is to import nothing but B-grade, C-grade, and Z-grade horror movies, or weird, artistic, philosophical love stories.

"God, nobody dreams anymore," I sigh.

Recently I saw Molly Ringwald in a movie. The young star of *Pretty in Pink* had turned into a frumpy, middle-aged actress playing some desperate femme fatale. I got so excited I cried out, "Molly! How've you been? Look what we've come to, huh?" and immediately put the movie on our order list. I could hear my coworkers muttering that I'm out of touch, old-fashioned, trying to restore my virginity, or whatever, but I didn't care.

"Listen, those first time movies are going to be popular again real soon, you wait and see," I told them. "True love is back in style. You know, like when the guy unbuttons the girl's blouse for the first time, and she starts to breathe heavily, and she's shaking with fear and rapture . . . That's what it's all about. That's sensuality."

My coworkers stared at me in bewilderment, but I just turned my back on them, marched off to my desk, and sank my teeth self-righteously into my sandwich.

I can still remember all the words to the *Paradise* theme song. When I hum it to my reflection in the computer screen, I feel like I'm back in high school.

Just take my hand, it's paradise . . .

I'm the boss's girlfriend, I thought to myself, as I strutted around so nonchalantly that day.

As usual, work was hectic at the end of the month, but now things are a little quieter, I decide to have a word with our office manager about the schedule for the next few months.

"Ah, Moriko, just the person I wanted to see. Mind if we have a little chat?"

He takes me out of the office to the local Renoir coffee shop and tells me I'm to be laid off at the end of next month—corporate restructuring, apparently. What the fuck . . . ?

We leave the coffee shop, and the office manager goes off somewhere. I march to the convenience store, planning to buy a few magazines for work while I'm out of the office, but somehow I leave the store carrying a huge plastic bag filled with pens, tape, garbage bags, and envelopes. With a jolt, I realize I seem to be preparing to clear my desk. I slam the shopping bag angrily against the elevator doors and let out a wail. A loose strand of hair from my ponytail grazes my cheek.

What's going on?

Who the hell decided this?

It must be a mistake! Aono!

Aono is still overseas, attending a movie awards ceremony and then traveling around a few countries to buy up new works.

I have more and more egg dreams. The situation is always different, but every time someone gives me an egg, and every time I break it.

"Moriko, when's your period?" asks Mikami. We're in Shibuya, sitting side by side at the counter of our second bar of the night, crouched under the low ceiling. The counter is made of thick, black wood, the color of a river flowing through the night.

"Period?" The word leaves a frown on my face.

"Yeah, your period." Mikami frowns back at me. We're on our third drink, and have pretty much emptied a bottle of wine. "My wife just had a baby last fall, so I know all about that stuff now. I'll calculate it for you," he says. I must have told him about my plan to have a Year-of-the-Horse daughter. I tell him when my period is due, and he stares up at the ceiling for a while, deep in drunken thought. "Okay . . . so if you have sex in the first week of March, you should be able to get pregnant. Then, if all goes well and you get fertilized and the egg gets implanted, you'll give birth just in time, about December 20." The whites of his eyes shine egg-yolk yellow under the bar lights. I sigh, thinking that a child born on December 20 would be Sagittarius, which is incompatible with me. Suddenly, Mikami whacks me on the shoulder. "Hey, now's your chance! Aren't you glad you came drinking with me tonight?" He smirks, with his mouth full of wine. "So have you got anyone lined up to provide the seed for this daughter? You can have sex with me in the first week of March, if you like."

The black counter, with its patina of alcohol, smoke, and grease, looks up at us with a hard, cold, cynical gaze, as if bored at having to spend yet another night listening to a man and woman toss the same old platitudes back and forth. As I tap my fingers on the wooden surface, Mikami nudges me with his shoulder and orders another drink, raising a finger to the waiter behind the bar. I follow the finger with my eyes, and as I watch its subtle movements, I begin to imagine its skill in other areas. Then I chuckle to myself, thinking that there's no particular skill involved in fertilization.

Aono is still out of town, and this is my first night out in ages. Recently Rei has stopped going out with me. Apparently she called me a dirty old bitch or something. But Rei is so young, and she never has any money. I always have to treat her, or at least go dutch, and what with me being unemployed now (or at least from the month after next), I'm really not too interested in going out with her either.

"Hey, you know how to fix the sex of your baby?" asks Mikami. "Everyone thinks it's all about what you eat and what position you have sex in, right? But actually, the most important thing is whether

The Unfertilized Egg

or not you're exposed to electromagnetic waves. So if you stare at a computer screen all day, you're more likely to have a girl. Bet you didn't know that, huh? I saw it on the Discovery Channel. Trust me—I'm a systems engineer, so I can pretty much guarantee you your Year-of-the-Horse daughter."

"Really?" I laugh, delightedly. "So what's your blood type? . . . B ? Oh God, you're perfect! A top stud!" We edge closer together, so that our cheeks are almost touching. I'm drunk, and starting to get a little turned on. I look down into my glass and wonder if I could get away with saying that the child was Aono's. Not likely, since we're not even fucking. I could just make up some crazy story. Virgin birth? Aerial transmission? But we're not talking pollen here, so that probably wouldn't work.

"Gimme your dandelion seeds," I slur out loud, laughing at my own joke as I slump over the counter. And then I notice that Mikami has disappeared. The bastard! Just a second ago he was stroking my ass and talking about going to a hotel to practice his fertilization techniques on me. What a tease! He had no intention of actually fucking me. All he wanted was a few drinks and a bit of dirty talk. Yeah, so his wife just gave birth. So what? Happy *birth*day, doting Daddy . . . Wimp. Pretends he's unsheathing his sword, then puts it back into its scabbard and runs off. Not exactly the way of the samurai . . . The check is lying quietly next to my elbow. His parting gift—the fucking freeloader. Looks like I'll be paying for his new baby celebrations, then.

I hand over a ten-thousand yen note and a five-thousand yen

note, and receive a few coins in return. I get on the last train to Toritsu Daigaku. No way I can afford a taxi the rest of the way home. After I've bought an apple juice at the convenience store, I'm left with exactly zero yen. For a moment I'm filled with delight at having enough money, but then realize with horror how quickly I've gotten used to my abject existence. I stagger back to my building and look up at the dark, square window of my apartment. Of all the windows in the block, only mine looks like a gloomy cave—a reflection of the hopeless life of the woman who lives there. I don't want to go in. What's going to happen to me now? Where am I going to work? How am I going to pay the rent? And what about when I get old and find myself at death's door? . . . Once more I'm alone in my filthy apartment, surrounded by the mounds of garbage. Without undressing, I climb into bed, and fall asleep on top of my magazines. No one will cross the threshold of my spider's cave tonight. The iron gate will remain locked. And I'll be alone, forever.

As I sleep, I become aware that the flower below my belly has unfurled its damp petals. I feel myself enfolded by walls dripping with moisture. I am sitting on something round, maybe a water bed. After a while, I notice that the water bed is actually the center of a rafflesia flower, and I realize that I am sitting on my own vulva. The sticky, fresh flower juice on my skin gives off an overpowering smell. Is this my own scent? I'm surrounded by quivering petals, and my face and body are covered in yellow pollen. A white egg appears in the air and falls into my open palm.

Hold it tightly! Tightly but gently, barks a voice.

The Unfertilized Egg

Tightly but gently? I look down at the egg which is still slightly warm, as though it has just been laid, and I am suffused with feelings of compassion and affection. The wetly glistening egg is round, white, innocent, yet somehow erotic, and suddenly I want to take it in my mouth or rub it gently over my nipples.

That is the egg that you will lay, says the voice. I look up, cupping the egg in my hands.

In the first week of March, proclaims the voice.

I sent an e-mail to Aono, but again there's no reply. I kick the birthday garbage by the front door, curse, and then set off for work feeling vaguely unpleasant, as if a bloody sanitary napkin were stuck to my underwear. I'm dressed in my usual, classy, single-working-woman style: blue scarf, tight black skirt, black boots, and carrying a tan shoulder bag in distressed leather. I walk along with my nose in the air, but my stiletto heels keep getting caught in the cracks in the sidewalk, making me lose my balance from time to time.

The silver train reflects the glare of the morning sun so that the whole station appears bathed in egg-yolk yellow. Somehow I manage to squeeze myself into the packed carriage. Through the window, beyond the hand straps, a green iron bridge stretches away into the distance.

You look like Diane Lane, did you know that?

Aono and I are in a taxi in the middle of the night. As we approach a green iron bridge, he touches my cheek.

"Diane Lane? If Diane Lane was Japanese, she'd be in a trashy Tuesday night suspense drama on TV. What are you trying to say? That I look like some actress on a trashy TV suspense drama?"

I'm annoyed, but Aono creases up with laughter. His fingers on my cheek are hot from the alcohol. We sit in traffic under the bridge, and I know that the sudden urge I feel to kiss him is a knee-jerk reaction that dates from my youth. When Diane Lane was young, she didn't look like an actress in a trashy TV suspense drama. More than twenty years ago, I saw *A Little Romance* in a movie theater in Yokohama. I ate an ice-cream sandwich that tasted of wet drawing paper, and sipped on a cola full of ice. Thirteen-year-old Diane Lane skipped across the screen in a denim skirt, hand in hand with a boy. They ran away to Venice because they'd heard that if two people kiss under the Bridge of Sighs at sunset, their love will last forever.

I was so young then, scared of even holding a boy's hand in gym class, and wondering if I would ever fall in love. The movie blew me away, and that sunset kiss was sewn into my heart. Decades have passed, but even now, whenever I pass under a bridge with a man, I always think that I'd better kiss him, just to be sure. Yeah, I know it's corny. So corny it's scary. I can't remember how many men I've kissed under bridges, swearing undying love (not out loud of course, and not because I meant it, but because the occasion seemed to demand it). Sometimes the kiss even turned into a groping session, soiling the memory of *A Little Romance*. But neither the kisses nor the groping sessions ever brought about the miracle of undying love.

The Unfertilized Egg

I look up at Aono and see that he is right in the middle of a huge yawn. He mutters groggily that he wants to go for noodles.

This is the first time I've been away from him for so long. The company is functioning smoothly without its president, but I miss him. I miss his cute, boyish face when he's fooling around, and the way his chiseled profile hints at stubbornness when he's silent. There are just two weeks left until the first week of March, but I don't even know if he'll be back by then. Unconsciously, I grip my left hand gently with my right. I am holding an egg made of air. This time I manage not to break it.

What's going to happen to my B-type, Year-of-the-Horse egg?

Uchiki sidles up to me and asks if I'm free after work tonight. My train of thought is broken, and I clench my fist. The soft, brown, wavy hair curling over his forehead reminds me of a Danish pastry, and I realize suddenly that I'm hungry. I didn't eat breakfast this morning. For the last few days, I've eaten nothing but tapioca and coconut milk at home. I haven't been shopping, and I've used up everything in my freezer. Uchiki is waiting for an answer, so I give him a quick nod, get up from my desk, and go to the coffee shop on the first floor.

It's ten fifteen, so they're still serving breakfast. I order a boiled egg, cabbage salad, and toast. At a table in the corner, surrounded by fake palm trees and warmly bathed in sunlight, I feel myself relax. I take a sip of thin, watery coffee and then set to work on the boiled egg in its small cup. I imagine it when it was raw, rolling around like an innocent child. But now, boiled, it sits there sullenly, pretending to be asleep. The rough white shell feels like textured paper. I break it on the rim of the cup, and that's when I remember—

I broke the egg I was holding in my dream.

I peel away the shell carefully to reveal the succulent, white flesh. I sprinkle some salt and take a bite. The warm yolk sticks obstinately to my teeth. As I scrape away the thick, sticky substance with my tongue and wash it down with a mouthful of coffee, it occurs to me that this stubborn boiled egg is a noble food, a whole complex life contained within its shell. It was the soul of the egg that clung so determinedly to my teeth.

When I was in elementary school, I kept budgerigars. I had a breeding pair, but one day the male escaped, and after that, for some reason, the female began to lay eggs one after another, as if to spite him. None of them hatched; they all rotted. I remember thinking how big the eggs were in relation to the budgie's body, and how hard it must be for her to lay them, her whole body swollen as she strained with all her might. In winter, I put the birdcage in the garden shed, and she would sit on her nest all day, silently warming the eggs, never singing, never flying. Birds don't have facial expressions, and their eyes do nothing but blink, so I never knew what she was thinking. Perhaps she felt lonely or frustrated as she sat there, her black eyes darting about. Maybe she missed her lover. I guess birds aren't capable of such varied emotions, so it was probably just instinct that made her keep on laying those useless eggs. They smelled bad when they rotted, but whenever I tried to clean out the nest, she would fly into a rage and peck my finger. It hurt, and I was scared, and after that I kind of gave up taking care of her . . .

I realize that I've been sitting over my breakfast for thirty minutes, and hurry back to the office.

After work, I go for a drink with Uchiki and two younger girls, just the four of us. We end up in a cheap restaurant next to the Parco department store in Shibuya. The sweet vapor of warm sake and the smell of charred chicken fat permeate the restaurant and put us all in a good mood. I usually avoid socializing with my coworkers, because I know that accidentally spilling the beans about me and Aono would be as easy as accidentally spilling my drink.

"Come here often, then?" I ask.

"Uh . . . yeah." The girls shoot conspiratorial glances at each other and snigger.

Rude bitches. No sooner have we said cheers than they start digging their chopsticks into every dish on the table at such speed you'd think they had a thousand hands each. They chew ponderously on the meat and graze on the salad like horses. Their lips glisten with fat, taking on an erotic, meaty color. They remind me of buxom young milkmaids standing in a meadow. I bet they lay good eggs: free-range, and dark brown rather than white. And I bet they don't care about all the wasted eggs they've laid up until now, knowing that sooner or later they'll snare a good man and get themselves fertilized.

The wrinkles at the corners of Aono's eyes are creased with pleasure. It always amazes me that a grown man can look so vulnerable.

He is on top of me. Suddenly, he lets out a loud groan and stops moving. "Hell, Moriko, for a moment there I thought I'd come," he says, looking as if he is about to cry.

"Of course you haven't, don't worry," I say, comforting him but secretly feeling a little upset at having been interrupted so abruptly. I jump up and stroke the sheets. "See? Nothing there." How can I possibly tell him I want him to get me pregnant, while I stand here imitating a naked kindergarten teacher? Maybe next time I could deceive him into thinking he didn't come. But no, that would be too cowardly. I look down at Aono's flaccid penis and imagine its thoughts:

My life doesn't get any easier, you know. These days, it's hard enough just to know whether I've come or not.

Well, I can't go asking him to waste his precious seed for the sake of my own selfish whims.

I sip my drink, lost in thought. Uchiki looks over at me, as if he wants to say something.

"What?"

"Nothing. I'll tell you later."

We leave the restaurant at ten, and go our separate ways. The two girls walk off together to catch their train. I wander down the hill, buy a can of juice, and take a deep swig. My cell phone announces the arrival of a text message. It's from Uchiki, just as I expected.

We go to a cheap bar. A group of tall, middle-aged white guys stand by the door, their cheeks shining pink like decorative lighting.

I feel as though I'm making my way through a forest as I squeeze past them. A country band is playing a live set in the corner. Lanterns hang down from the ceiling. The pretty young girl behind the bar wears an unattractive scowl. We buy five-hundred-yen beers and drink them standing up.

"I heard you're quitting," says Uchiki. The egg-and-potato quiche I ordered is too greasy and tastes terrible. I contemplate the marinated sardines for my next course.

"I'm not quitting—I've been fired," I shout angrily. I'm glad the bar is noisy.

"Have you got another job lined up? What are you going to do?"

"I have no fucking idea."

Didn't I have this conversation with someone else not so long ago?

Got someone to fertilize you lined up?

Got another job lined up?

My life is driven by these ever-more desperate questions. And the only person who can help me has gone away, and who knows when he's coming back.

". . . haven't you?" Lost in my thoughts again, I haven't been listening to Uchiki.

"I know you've been seeing the boss, haven't you? If that's all over, how about getting together with me?"

Uchiki is working hard to present my egg with his young sperm. I don't know if he's embarrassed, or just drunk, but his eyes are misted over and he looks like some innocent virgin. The rafflesia petals deep down below begin to writhe. The swollen, fleshy gateway opens wider in anticipation of imminent fertilization, urging him onward.

"What's your blood type?" I gasp, as our bodies bang together. His smell fills my nostrils, and I feel his heart beating fast.

"B," he says. The sound comes bursting out of his mouth. My egg itches with anticipation and rolls around in my uterus like a ball on a roulette wheel. *Only nine days left*, it reminds me. I know. I know. But I want Aono's sperm. I look up at Uchiki, and he seems far away. Maybe it's because he's tall, or maybe it's the angle. His hard skin feels young and fresh, and his veins stand up as if he is angry. Something isn't right. I'm not comfortable. I twist my body left and right, trying to escape from his grip. But no matter how I try, his cock stays firmly in place and I can't disengage myself from it. I hear a voice urging, *Go for it!* After a while, heat begins to gather in the core of my body, and the petals creep closer together in preparation. *Don't spill it*, the voice calls out.

"Moriko, I'm getting close."

The sound of his voice takes me by surprise, and I open my mouth. Uchiki fills it with his cock, and a second later with his bitter, astringent semen. There is a brief silence.

The Unfertilized Egg

My rafflesia sighs disappointedly.

Uchiki whispers something contentedly, and falls on top of me.

For me, it just felt all wrong from beginning to end.

iii

In my dream, I am being subjected to some kind of medieval French punishment. I am tied to a wooden pole in a town square. Someone is banging a gong, and a crowd of people are throwing stones at me. I am being stoned to death. Wait, they're not stones— they're eggs! They come flying through the air and break as they hit my body. In an instant, I am covered in sticky yellow liquid. I stink of raw eggs, and have to close my eyes. "Stop! Stop! Don't waste all those eggs! I can't catch them all!" My misplaced screams of protest fall on deaf ears. An eerie marbled pattern of egg yolk and blood appears before my eyes, and I swoon . . . I wake up and my panties are wet. Was that supposed to be a sex dream?

No e-mail from Aono today either. Instead, my last message to him has come back undelivered. I wonder where he is. Somebody at the office must know, but how can I ask? I'm almost late, and I rush to the door, kicking the garbage on my way out. Chocolate truffles spill out of a paper bag onto the floor. I step on one. Red jelly seeps out and sticks to my shoe.

Eight days left to the first week of March.

The two girls from the restaurant are running around spreading rumors about me and Uchiki. Uchiki looks up at me meaningfully and walks over. He shows me a document relating to some business that could easily have been left until tomorrow, just so he can get a good look at me. Fucking idiot. Have I still got cum on my face or something? I think of Kristy McNichol, Tatum O'Neal, and all those other coming-of-age movie stars. How would they have eased their way out of such an awkward situation? I wish I had that white ten-gallon hat that Kristy McNichol wore in *The Night the Lights Went Out in Georgia*, where she played a young singer traipsing around the countryside and taking care of her useless brother. I would put it on and stride out of the office. I'd probably get away with it. "Aw, it's so sad, the office spinster getting fired so suddenly. She's obviously gone crazy," they'd say. One morning years and years ago, I cut high school and watched *The Night the Lights Went Out in Georgia* at a movie theater in Yokohama. I'd have gotten into trouble if someone had caught me wandering around town in my school uniform, so I hid out in the theater until dusk and watched the movie twice in a row. I did the same thing when I watched *One from the Heart*, with Nastassja Kinski playing an acrobat in a winged leotard.

It seems the company president is to return next week. Apparently he has an important appointment, and everyone figures there's no way he'll be able to miss it.

"Have you heard why the boss has been away for so long?" asks one of my younger female colleagues.

"No, I haven't," I reply.

"Everyone's saying he got Risa from advertising pregnant."

Seven days left to the first week of March.

Six days left to the first week of March.

Five days left to the first week of March.

I call a few companies, but I don't even get an interview. Well, it's not exactly as if I'm busting a gut to find a new job. I don't care. I guess I'm lacking a sense of emergency about the whole situation, acting as though someone has merely plunged my face into a basin of warm water so I can't breathe for a second, when in reality, I've been abandoned on the ocean floor without an aqualung. I'm living in dreamland. It's funny how those first time movies and true love stories of the eighties still have me in their grip. I suppose those young girls are almost past their sell-by date now, just like me, but I always think of them as naive teenagers, singing love songs over my shoulder, licking ice cream, and smiling. They link their arms through mine, and for some reason I feel that I can relax; that there is still time.

My apartment is becoming filthier by the day. I can't seem to motivate myself to clean, or wash my clothes, or shop for food. I can't remember the last time I bothered to open the windows. Musty air coils around my bedroom, mingling with the stench of my sweat-stained T-shirt. A bowl of ancient, abandoned chili beans sits on the kitchen counter. The spices give off a smell like the body odor of a middle-aged man. It reminds me of Aono.

I was thirty-two when I started dating Aono. I was so clueless and carefree then, and I had no idea which direction to take in life. It was Aono who took my hand and guided me, step by step. But after about six months the whole thing began to drive me crazy. I felt choked up with loneliness, and wanted to scream at the unfairness of it all. My frustration led me to an unmarried guy around my age, but Aono refused to let me go. One day we arranged to meet at a discreet little coffee shop near the office. When I arrived, Aono was already waiting. I'll never forget his face that day. It was drawn and dark, full of pent-up emotion. He looked at me pleadingly and said, "Moriko, don't mess me around, okay?" He gripped my cold fingers, and I knew I would never do anything to hurt him again. If my story were a true love movie, this would be the happy ending. But our long, long ending dragged on for another four years.

Three days left to the first week of March.

Two days left to the first week of March.

Every night I dream of eggs.

I am sleeping naked on top of the bed sheets. I open my legs, clench my thigh muscles, and press down. There's a huge egg filling my cave. The egg is pressing against the walls of the cave, trying to push its way out, but the walls resist, pulsating rapidly against the pressure and intense pain.

"It's too big! It'll never get out." Tears trickle down, but I know I have to keep going. I exhale deeply, and the walls quiver again. I can see the blood running through the back of my eyelids. The walls engulf me.

As I am expelled, I cry out. "Look! You can see the head!"

First published, 2004
Translation by Philip Price

Junko Hasegawa was born in 1966. She is well-known in Japan for her regular appearances in a variety of magazines as a writer of "illustrated reports"; humorous, comic-strip style essays in which Hasegawa depicts the trials and tribulations of the generation of Japanese women to which she belongs. She has recently embarked on a career as a writer of fiction and essays. "The Unfertilized Egg" is taken from her first short story collection, *Germination*.

The Shadow of the Orchid

Nobuko Takagi

When she went into her son's room, his smell was still there. She thought it might be coming from the duvet. Every time she aired the bedding, the smell seemed to grow fainter.

Bed, desk, bureau—he had bought what he needed in Tokyo, so most of his furniture was just as he had left it. But with him gone, his room was swiftly fading into colorless, transparent space. Michiko worried that if this went on, her son would feel awkward when he came home on summer vacation. She wanted this house and this room to feel like his home base, and she wanted the apartment in Tokyo to feel like temporary lodging. But she knew her son would spend the next six years in Tokyo, and if he stayed longer, this room and this house might well become nothing more than memories for him.

The springs squealed when she sat down on the bed.

Great news about your son! Congratulations! You're so lucky! Everything went so smoothly! It must be such a relief!

If there were sincere words, there were also begrudging, biting words. Some friends had sympathized: *He must have felt terrific pressure, being the only son of a doctor.* But that son had chosen to go into medicine without regard to his father's profession. His father, Yukio, worked at a large hospital, so there was nothing to pass down. Their son would probably work at a hospital in Tokyo or another large city. His personality was like Yukio's, suited to research, so it was hard to imagine him starting his own practice.

His room got more sunlight than any other room in the house, so Michiko dried the laundry there on a folding rack. She would take a load from the dryer and hang just the items that were still damp. By afternoon they were nearly always dry. She took the white shirts and the cotton gloves she used for gardening from her son's room to the living room, where she tossed them lightly on top of a mountain of other laundry piled at the end of the sofa. Now she would fold them one by one.

For some reason, whenever Michiko immersed herself in this task, she would begin to feel herself losing gray matter, slowly but surely. If she thought about nothing at all, her hands would still roll the men's briefs into the shape of cabbage rolls, and locate the mates for the socks. Michiko knew she needed to keep using her head, but it refused to work when there was no need. At least when her son was at home she had to take each pair of briefs in her hand and judge whether it was his or Yukio's, but now even that was unnecessary. Folding laundry had become an increasingly mindless task.

Once she put the laundry away, she was free until evening. Whether the day was sunny or rainy, this time brought both happiness and loneliness. She could avoid boredom by turning on the television, but Michiko could not watch the afternoon shows for more than ten minutes at a time. Trivial incidents involving celebrities were hashed out like major world events, and male analysts knit their brows over concerns such as a housewife who shoplifted during her period. It quickly became too much.

Michiko did not for a moment think of herself as an exceptional woman. She felt she had average features and intelligence, thanks to her parents, but not only did she miss the point of gossip shows aimed at housewives, she felt something like soot collecting in her body when she watched. Lately she had begun to think it might be her age.

One more year. Only one more year until I'm fifty. She didn't care to hurry, but she couldn't help feeling that she had been pushed from behind, from a land of green grass to a rough place littered with rocks. She was grateful to have none of the health problems associated with the change of life; whatever else might happen, it seemed she would be able to face menopause in peace. But she sensed a draining of her mind and her body, and with her son's move to Tokyo, this sensation had grown more pronounced. Sometimes Michiko would feel she was the happiest person in the world and begin to cry. At other times, she would see herself as a woman of no value either to Yukio or to their son, and she would wish she could die and return her body to dust. Could any of this have to do with menopause?

Michiko turned on the television, then turned it off after the usual ten minutes. As she opened a women's magazine, her limbs grew heavy, and she lay down to rest on the sofa. Unsure whether she was sleepy or not, she closed her eyes, then opened them again just a little. Pale pinks and purples shone at the center of her narrowed field of vision. It looked as though countless butterflies were opening and closing their wings in a haze. Michiko hurriedly opened her eyes wide, to see something Yukio had brought home a week before: a dendrobium orchid plant in full bloom.

Michiko's heart began to pound. All week, without fail, when she and the orchid had found themselves alone together in the afternoons, her heart had reacted strangely. Nothing happened when she reexamined the plant with a guest who gasped at the lovely flowers, or when she and Yukio sat watching television at night, the flowerpot between them. But when Michiko was alone with the plant, something happened. She was seized by an emotion that was hard to explain, something like deep impatience. Calling this hard to explain was the easy way out. When she thought about it honestly, the cause became perfectly clear: she was jealous of the orchid.

One of Yukio's patients was a young woman with cancer of the kidneys. Yukio, a kidney specialist, had been her doctor since she was in middle school, when she suffered from frequent bacterial infections. Her kidney function would drop below normal, but she always seemed to recover well enough to return to everyday life.

Chronic illness of the kidneys is difficult to cure. Yukio said that when this patient didn't show up at the hospital for a while, he would feel glad knowing she was managing day by day. At the same time, he would worry she was slowly losing ground. His worry proved to be well-founded: when the patient appeared in Yukio's office in her early twenties, after an absence of several years, cancer had spread through her kidneys and lungs. For exactly three and a half years after the cancer was found, she lived.

Yukio rarely spoke to Michiko about the dozens of patients in his care, but he seemed to feel very regretful about this one. When he first learned the cancer was at an advanced stage, and later when treatments didn't go well, there were times when he would uncharacteristically complain: "Why does it have to take such a pretty girl?"

Michiko had often heard Yukio's colleagues use similar words. One friend, a surgeon, observed that boys with bone cancer who had to have a leg amputated always seemed to have a gentle nature and eyes like angels. Michiko did not believe that sympathy and compassion created this impression; she, too, felt disease somehow chose young people with pure hearts and clear eyes.

So when Yukio first started referring to this patient as a "pretty girl," Michiko pictured a child in her teens and felt sympathy. But the child had become a woman in her early twenties, and even though she had been a patient since middle school, Michiko began to notice when Yukio kept calling her a pretty girl.

"So, the woman you mentioned, how is she?" When Michiko asked, Yukio poured out a list of the patient's painful symptoms, as though relieved that he had finally found someone who would listen. Michiko shook her head. "Imagine getting such a terrible disease before falling in love or marrying . . . Poor thing, she must have struggled since her teens to live normally. God isn't fair."

"That's why I am now her doctor, father, and lover."

Yukio was the same age as Michiko, but he had just declared himself to be the patient's father and lover without a second thought. After his words sank in, Michiko sensed her husband losing his composure just a little.

She tried to sweep the whole incident under the rug, including Yukio's show of feeling. But now and then she would find herself stopping to catch her breath at the thought of this young woman, who had moved a man near fifty to call himself her lover.

"Well, aren't you lucky, receiving so much trust as her doctor? If she has no one else to lean on, you must be her whole world." Michiko poked Yukio's jaw with her finger, like an elder sister scolding him for teasing. He would have to keep caring for the woman's heart, as well as her kidneys, now, wouldn't he, she added. These words were perfectly sincere. Michiko was not a bit surprised by the idea that a doctor would be more than just a doctor in the eyes of female patients whose hearts had weakened with their bodies.

Then, only a week ago, the woman had died. Yukio had come home that night with the dendrobium in his arms. He said she had given it to him. This orchid, which produced many flowers on one round stem, was apparently easier to care for than moth orchids or cattleya. Yukio said it had sat on the windowsill in the woman's hospital room for several years. At first it must have been a get-well present from someone. Although the original flowers eventually died, the plant would bloom again every spring with proper care, so to the woman, it had probably been more than a source of comfort—it must have become a reason for living.

The flowers on the dendrobium Yukio brought home were half in bloom and half in bud. The woman must have kept watch until the plant flowered again this year, then died. Attached to the flowerpot was a scrap of paper torn from a notebook. On it were written instructions for caring for the dendrobium. According to these instructions, one could keep the plant inside, watering moderately, as long as the flowers were in bloom. If the base of the stem produced new shoots after the flowers finished, there would be flowers the next year, so one should provide plenty of light and fertilizer. At the end of the note, round, childish characters said, *Doctor, care for these flowers as you would care for me.*

"I'm not sure I can do it," Michiko said. "Those cymbidiums we were given haven't budded even once. I don't have a green thumb." In a corner of their yard lay three or four pots of cymbidium orchids that were nothing but leaves, and half of those had wilted for lack of water.

"It doesn't matter. Accepting her gift was the important part." Yukio didn't seem to attach much importance to the wishes of the deceased.

Two days after they placed the pot on a low table between two pieces of the sofa set, the flowers reached full bloom. They were so vivid it almost felt as though the life lost in the hospital had erupted in the living room. The plant had also come into the house shortly after their son left for Tokyo. Whatever the reason, Michiko couldn't help feeling that the orchid was more than an ordinary plant.

She could not believe that Yukio and the woman had been

anything more than doctor and patient. That the woman had cher-ished feelings for Yukio as a member of the opposite sex seemed certain. But Michiko believed that as a doctor, Yukio had seen the woman through to the end of her life while skillfully managing her moods. To Michiko, he had never betrayed emotional attachment to the woman beyond saying she was a pretty girl. Then again, the night she died, Yukio had stood for a long time at the mirror after his bath, examining the naked upper half of his body.

Catching Michiko as she passed behind him, he had thrust out his chest before the mirror and demanded to know where and how he looked different from a man in his twenties. At the time, Michiko couldn't really see much difference, but that was probably because his skin was glistening from the bath. When she thought of it again the next day, there were white strands mixed into her husband's hair, and the corners of his eyes sagged, as did his cheeks and his neck. As he often bragged, his weight had not changed since he was about thirty, but age was definitely catching up. Of course, it was Michiko who had started to show signs of aging first, even though she and Yukio had been born in the same year.

That time in front of the mirror, what was Yukio really thinking? Did he vaguely wish he had behaved like a man in his twenties? She doubted he really felt bad about failing to respond to any wishes the woman might have had, but a feeling close to that seemed to be toying with his heart. Every time she sat on the sofa and looked at those flowers, she would begin to see a young woman lying in bed in a hospital room. She would see Yukio look into her eyes, grasp her hand, expose her chest, and place his stethoscope on her breasts. At that point, Michiko's heart would start its pounding. She knew the body of a person near death is not beautiful, as in the movies; even the body of a Hollywood actress would make you want to look away. But Michiko had never seen this woman with her own eyes; even on her deathbed, she flaunted the beauty of a woman in her twenties.

"What's wrong with you? Not enough sleep?" Yukio asked, tightening his necktie. While removing his suit from the wardrobe, Michiko had been overcome by a sensation resembling dizziness and involuntarily sat on the bed nearby. She rubbed her eyes. Come to think of it, he was right: she wasn't sleeping enough. She couldn't fall asleep at night, and in the morning her eyes would open while it was still dark outside. She would go to the toilet, wander into the living room and gaze into the fish tank, then return to bed after confirming the presence of the dendrobium, whose reflection swayed in the aquarium like fronds of seaweed. No deep sleep awaited her after that. Sometimes sleep would beckon about thirty minutes before it was time to get up, but Michiko's slumber would soon be abruptly cut off, and it would be as hard to wake up as it had been to fall asleep.

"People say not being able to sleep soundly is a sign of age. Is that true, medically speaking?" she asked.

"People say that. But if the human body gets tired, it'll sleep, whether you want it to or not. It's not age—probably lack of exercise."

"I wonder if I should take up yoga again."

"It's probably a sign that you were using more energy on our son than on me. Now that he's gone, you have less to do."

"That's not true. Even when he was here, the washing machine did the washing, and the vacuum sweeper did the sweeping."

"Then it must be labor of the heart. Anxiety. You were completely on edge while he was preparing for entrance exams, and now he's gone."

"I bet you want to tell me I have one of those 'diseases of affluence,' don't you?"

"Nope. More like a disease of happiness."

"You must think I don't have a thing in the world to fret about."

"Well, do you?"

"No, nothing in particular." It wasn't nothing, exactly, but if she put it into words, her malady was sure to be classified as a disease of affluence or a disease of happiness. A hollow had opened in Michiko's heart, and every time she looked into the mirror and found new wrinkles in her neck, or failed to recall the name of a longtime acquaintance, or realized she was puffing and panting when she climbed a flight of stairs, the hollow grew wider than before. But it was no use trying to put back what was lost; she knew that she needed to reach out to the future.

"Must be the springtime blues," Michiko said, then laughed. "That thing they call 'melancholy when the trees are in bud.' I wonder if my balance is a little off—like in adolescence. This must be the period when I wonder what to do with myself, now that my men have gone far, far away."

"The only one who's gone far away is our son. I'm right here. Say, are you up for a second adolescence tonight?" Now that Michiko had finally managed to stand, Yukio drew her toward him by the waist, then briskly released her and headed for the front door.

After Michiko finished tidying up and read the paper, she made her daily phone call to check on her mother, who lived nearby. Nothing new was usually the reply, but today Michiko had to spend fifteen minutes listening to an account of a battle her mother was having with the dentist over some problem with her false teeth. When Michiko finally put down the receiver, the dendrobium was standing over her like a flowering tree. And again, for some reason, her chest grew tight, and she could hear the words, *Doctor, care for me*.

Michiko had thought menopausal disorders had nothing to do with her, but now she wasn't so sure. She scooped up the dendrobium, went to her son's room, and put the pot on his desk. From here, it couldn't catch her eye. Michiko reasoned she could return it to the living room when it was time for Yukio to come home. Feeling as though one important matter had been put to rest, Michiko ate last night's leftovers for lunch. Reminding herself that this was heaven, heaven, she lay down on the sofa. But suddenly she felt uneasy, as though she was about to lose her son, as though the hand of a dangerous woman was reaching toward him. She got to her feet again.

Removing the pot from her son's room, she cast about for a place to put it, then opened the sliding glass door that led to the yard and put it outside. The sky was completely clear, and a breath of fresh spring air blew in through the door. Michiko decided she would bring the pot inside before the evening grew chilly. Again she lay down on the sofa.

She closed her eyes but saw brightness. Were her optic nerves really capturing the color of blood and tissue, or was she having a fantasy with a color all its own? If her optic nerves were mechanically capturing the color, she would expect it to be homogenous and fixed. But when she varied the level and direction of her focus, reds became rich purples or light pinks, and a wavelike form appeared in one direction. Yes, this must be a fantasy . . .

Then all at once, against a vivid red background, a black silhouette appeared. She sensed something slipping between her closed eyes and the light, and its shadow soaking into her eyelids.

Michiko carefully followed that shadow.

The shadow was quite complex. First, in its exact middle was something resembling a single stem; above that hovered a blur in the shape of a woman's head. When Michiko trained her eyes on the blur, she could make out different layers of petals: pale outer petals in a single layer surrounding a small cluster of thick inner petals.

I knew it, thought Michiko, opening her eyes. Before her was the woman's face.

"How did you get inside?" Michiko asked, first of all. She was sure she had closed the sliding door. The woman turned around and looked at the door. It was open just enough for her body to slip through. "Tell me, what is your name?" Michiko asked. "I have a feeling my husband told me, but lately I even forget the names of my own acquaintances."

"Anything's fine. If you like, call me Denko."

"Ah, Den as in dendrobium . . . I see. I'll use Denko if you say you don't mind, but the very idea that a tragic, young beauty would have a heavy, plodding name like Denko! It makes you sound denser— I mean . . . less refined than you are. Then again, everything with an outside has an inside. There's probably more to you than your looks."

Sitting up, Michiko inspected Denko. Her hair was much as the shadowy vision behind Michiko's eyelids had suggested: a soft, voluminous, chestnut-colored mass, carefully braided behind her ears. Her forehead was wide, giving the impression of intelligence and wit; her body was plump, reminiscent of tropical warmth. She seemed healthy, but even so, she would lose her fight with cancer.

Her lips were a purplish red, exactly like the heart of one of the orchid's flowers; the upward slant of the corners of her mouth also seemed less like part of a human body than something transplanted from the orchid. She was more of a funny face than a beauty, which made Michiko feel slightly better.

"I should be inviting you in politely, but my feelings are a bit complicated, you know."

"I know. Suddenly things have come this far. I hardly expect you to welcome me."

"No, no, you're very welcome. Looking at something lovely always makes me feel good."

The Shadow of the Orchid

"Is that really the truth?"

"Not exactly, but I am making an effort to think it is. Anyway, let's settle down. You sit over there."

Denko sat down catty-corner from Michiko, drawing her knees to her chest. Her white skin absorbed so much light from the room that it seemed nearly ready to burst; when she shifted her knees even a little to the side, her long legs gleamed. One of Michiko's friends had lamented that people in their twenties are still the same height as people in their forties, but their legs are ten centimeters longer than before; now I see, Michiko thought. Denko's right and left breasts protruded at exactly the same height, as though a rubber ball had been divided and the halves affixed.

"Actually I—" As Michiko began to speak, Denko leaned forward and cut her off.

"I wish you wouldn't say it that way, like a confession. I'm bad with heavy talk. I haven't taken part in any serious discussions since I was in the hospital." Denko's round eyes darted busily as she spoke. Her legs had begun to jiggle up and down. Perhaps she didn't like sitting still.

"Very well. I'll say this lightly, so you take it lightly."

"Go on."

"It's about my husband."

"My doctor. What about him?"

"What happened between the two of you? Did anything happen? I've been having some thoughts, probably pointless . . ."

Denko's eyes flashed maliciously, and her mouth twitched.

Michiko instantly wished she hadn't mentioned anything.

"Between me and the doctor, you say?"

"Oh, never mind. It doesn't matter either way."

"But I do mind. What are you saying about me and the doctor?"

"You were patient and physician, right?"

"Yes . . ."

"Was that all you were? That's what I wanted to ask, but really, it's okay."

"Look, why is it okay now? This is what I can't stand about adults. They never tell you what they really think, then they act so nasty later . . ." Denko spoke the last phrase like a coddled child. As Michiko listened, she began to pair this voice with that line of round characters: *Doctor, care for these flowers as you would care for me.* This voice lacked gravity and exuded a certain naïveté. Before now, Michiko had often tried to put a voice with the single line of writing, but the voice she had heard was rich and melancholy, full of sighs. That voice didn't actually exist. Michiko marveled at how one phrase could take on a variety of meanings, depending on the speaker.

"I know it's silly for someone of my age, but I suppose I'm jealous of you," Michiko said. "Lately, when I see young people, I've been feeling disagreeable, questioning my own existence. I knew it was just me, but I couldn't stop myself from getting depressed . . . Then my husband kept talking about you, and my delusions grew and grew."

"And now?"

"Oh, I'm fine now. I'm glad I met you. I think I may have been fretting over nothing, after all."

Denko slowly crossed her legs, which had been stretched out in front of her. She let out a long, adult sigh. "Hearing something like that depresses *me*, you know. I admired the doctor, and I depended on him for everything."

"Yes, I completely understand."

"You feel relieved because you met me and found out I'm not grown-up."

"Oh, you're very grown-up—dazzlingly so—but my worries have cleared up somehow. Lately, I've been letting the slightest things affect my mood, but finally I seem to be feeling better, so please don't say something that will upset me again."

"Can I ask you just one thing?" Denko said. She glanced up at Michiko, her lips pursed. She looked ready to protest, not probe.

"As you wish," Michiko said, still relaxed.

"I was wondering why the doctor's fingernails were always cut so nicely. I thought his wife must be cutting them for him every day after his bath. I was jealous of you, too, you know."

"His fingernails? Do you really think the wife cuts them one by one? This isn't the late nineteenth century. I've never really looked at his fingernails . . ."

"They were always cut very carefully in a curve, and filed . . ."

"Are you sure? I don't think we have a nail file in the house."

"I know because he told me himself. When he came by on his rounds, he would show me the fingers on both hands and ask if they looked acceptable. He would have this clownish expression on his face. He wouldn't start the exam until his nails had passed my inspection."

"He must have thought very highly of you, getting so worked up about his nails scratching you by mistake." As she replied, Michiko's emotions began to stir once more. When it came to Yukio's nails, just one memory came to mind. It was from when they first met, barely in their twenties. Before every date, Yukio would turn up with his nails cut almost to the quick, curved, and filed. Michiko herself only groomed her nails enough to get by; she had rarely even applied nail polish. So she was constantly amazed by the cleanliness of Yukio's nails. But once they married, he stopped paying them so much attention.

At first Michiko thought medical students must get scolded if they grew out their nails even a little. She later learned that was not the case. She also learned from Yukio himself that he had been cutting his nails before dates in preparation for a certain event. Michiko had laughed. "Why, you never used to behave that way at all! I thought you had no interest in my body!" Yukio replied glumly, "The body of a woman I had never touched was scary."

"Now that you mention it, my husband was always saying something to young people about fingernails. He even said it to our son: 'A doctor's fingertips are very important. The fingertips are the point of connection with a patient, so you must always keep the nails groomed.' I'm positive he used to say that." Michiko wasn't positive at all, but when she tried saying it aloud she could even envision

Yukio giving the advice to their son. He wasn't the sort of father who spoke about feelings, but he may well have spoken about fingernails.

"Sounds a little like *E.T.*, doesn't it?" Denko looked at Michiko skeptically.

"Oh yes—where the fingertips touch and there's a flash? I'm sure it's the same way with doctors. Now, is there anything else you want to ask?"

"No." Denko fell silent, as though driven back by the force of Michiko's determination.

"If not, I wish you'd go away."

"I will."

"But this isn't the end . . . If I want to meet you again, we can meet, right?"

"That should be okay. You seem to have a knack for conjuring up these fantasies."

Oh yes, that's right, fantasies. That was in a book I read recently. When a human tries to confirm her existence as an individual, they say it's vital for her to have her own personal fantasies. A person's physical makeup does *not* constitute individuality—everybody has two eyes, one nose, and one thyroid gland. If you put a couple of people in uniform and stand thirty meters away, you'll have no idea who's who. But fantasies are unique. The kind of fantasies a person embraces are supposed to determine who that person is. Yes, I'm sure about that book—it was written by a famous psychologist, and he said that fantasy could explain the mass movements of migratory birds . . . If you try to use science to explain why migratory birds fly certain places in certain seasons, you're almost certain to come up empty. But if we can understand the fantasies the birds embrace as a group, perhaps we can find . . .

No one was listening to Michiko's long exposition. She got up and looked at the clock. It was still rather early, but she opened the sliding door and brought the dendrobium inside. Not only were the flowers brilliant, they were also tenaciously strong, she observed; if she brushed one with a finger, she didn't leave a scar. She had heard the blooming period could last as long as a month. The glass side table bore a round mark from the pot, as though the orchid had left its stamp just there. Michiko placed the pot directly on the mark.

Yukio had not forgotten what he'd said to his wife when he left that morning. "I can't have you thinking all your men have run away," he said, reaching for Michiko in bed. Every time she took her husband's body into her own, Michiko thought of stitches binding two long pieces of fabric together. When she and Yukio were in their twenties, they had connected the pieces by coming together frantically again and again, but now, even without the physical act of seaming, the two pieces seemed to stay more or less aligned. Michiko doubted the two layers would ever be ripped apart, but even so, there was meaning in making visible stitches with needle and thread now and then. There was comfort, as well.

The length and strength of the stitches had hardly changed since Michiko and Yukio were first married. The stitches had simply gotten farther apart after the two of them entered their forties.

After they finished, Michiko didn't want Yukio to go right to sleep, so she talked to him. If she let him go, his loud snoring would begin in five minutes.

"Hey," she said, taking his hand in the dark. She felt his fingernails. They weren't exactly long, but it didn't feel like they had been cut recently. "Have you been cutting your fingernails properly?"

"Uh-huh."

"Have you been filing them, too?"

"Sometimes. Why?"

"Oh, no reason. I was just thinking, we don't have a nail file in the house." That didn't seem to bother Yukio, who was drifting off, still holding Michiko's hand. Hurriedly she yanked on it. "A long time ago, you used to cut your fingernails so short you almost hurt yourself. Remember?"

"Is that right? . . . Good night."

"Every date, I was amazed . . ."

"Did they hurt you? I'm sorry."

"Not at all—I just happened to remember. If you had a young lover now, I bet you would cut your fingernails very carefully before your dates," Michiko teased.

"I'm going to sleep now, okay?"

The darkness seemed to turn purple, as if she had closed her eyes. Michiko decided her husband was already lost in his fantasies, so she released his hand. As though he had been waiting for her to do so, he pulled away and turned over.

His head was undoubtedly filled with fantasies his wife could never imagine, but neither of them could ever glimpse the fantasies of the other, and she had begun to feel it might be the end of them if they did. Perhaps migratory birds have fantasies a group can share, but humans have no such thing. That's why they sometimes have to stitch themselves to each other, but even when they are in the midst of doing that, they can never cross over into the same fantasy world . . .

Michiko thought of her son. Through the act she and her husband had just performed, her son had formed inside her body, taken the shape of a human, come into the world, and grown up. Just now, he was probably in Tokyo drinking beer and watching a video. Suddenly, she couldn't see how any of this was real. If she didn't hold tight, perhaps even her son would disappear . . .

"So, we meet once more," Michiko said. Her own will was working far too much for this to be a dream. She had wished to meet Denko, so here she was.

"I wasn't sure if you'd call on me again," Denko said. "But thanks. I did think you might need me to convince yourself of your own happiness."

"It hurts when you put it that way. But it's probably true," Michiko replied. "I hate to admit it, but thinking of unhappy people is by far the quickest way to verify how happy I am. No one would ever say such a thing aloud, of course. I myself keep up the pretense of being above such things. But it's the truth. Just take a look at TV. Look at

The Shadow of the Orchid

women's weekly magazines, for that matter. The stories that sell are either the ones about princesses and actresses living fairy-tale lives, or the ones about the misery of the masses. People's hearts create those stories. They're a kind of fantasy, too."

"So, I'm the wretched woman who represents the misery of the masses."

That's exactly right, Michiko thought, but she grew tongue-tied and looked down at her hands. Her knuckles jutted up stiffly, the only part of her that looked witchlike. Denko's fingers were covered with delicate, transparent skin, which revealed veins, as in a leaf. Pink-colored blood percolated through them.

"So, are you feeling better now?" Denko asked.

"Yes, much better. Apparently they call this sort of ailment a 'phantom complaint,' but I have no one to complain to, so—"

"Go on, complain all you like. Nothing I hear can startle me now. Actually, I've been meaning to say thank you for the doctor's love."

"What did you just say?"

"I see the ailment of jealousy still troubles you."

"Please don't say hateful things that make me anxious. Lately I feel useless enough as it is, like a used car dumped on a scrap heap."

"This room is hot and stuffy. Perhaps you would be so kind as to take me out somewhere."

This room has grown hot and stuffy since *you* came, Michiko wanted to say.

"Where would you like to go?"

"To a time when the doctor was still young, when he had eyes without crow's-feet, a sharp Adam's apple, and a triangular chin . . ."

The Adam's apple of a doctor must loom large over someone looking up from a bed, Michiko thought. At the mirror, after his bath, Yukio had asked her where and how he looked different from a man in his twenties, but he should have asked Denko those questions. Don't they say people in their twenties look childlike nowadays, but they have a cool objectivity that is very adult? One of these days, Michiko would have to inform Yukio about his crow's-feet, his Adam's apple, and his chin.

She and Yukio had first met in Tokyo. Michiko took Denko to Shinjuku Gyoen Park. They walked through a place where crystalline sunlight spilled down through a stand of winter-wilted trees.

"When I was just about your age, I used to walk here with my husband. Both of us were still penniless students, so we were happy to find a place where you could pay the entrance fee and spend half a day. This was always our spot for dates . . . Yukio's horrible at singing, so he wasn't much for singalong cafes and the like. Oh, that's right—I feel a little odd talking about it, but on Saturdays we used to stay overnight in a hotel, then come into this park in the morning and lay together on the grass until evening. That was much later, of course."

"You must have been planning to get married, right?"

"I couldn't imagine being with anyone else, but I did have one dream of my own, you know. I wanted to be a translator."

"A doctor and a translator. That's so high-class it almost makes you dizzy, huh?"

The Shadow of the Orchid

"I married and moved away with him, so a dream it remained."

"You know, I like foreign mystery novels. I was always reading them in the hospital. The doctor liked mysteries, too."

"Oh, did my husband mention that, as well?"

Denko suddenly clammed up. Then she seemed to decide to spill the beans. The sunlight that slipped between the branches was dancing on her mass of chestnut-colored hair. Yukio had described her as a pretty girl, but her eyelashes were long, her eyes large, and her features more doll-like than human. This sort of face could well appear the same in death as in life, Michiko reflected.

"The doctor was kind enough to loan me all the mystery books he read. After I finished, I believe he took them home. I read all of the doctor's Dick Francis." Denko herself didn't seem to realize how much these few words would hurt Michiko. Determined not to let it show, Michiko pulled on her self-respect like a hat and raised her chin.

"No wonder the books my husband brought home from the hospital all seemed to have warped pages. Some of them even looked like they'd been wet. I remember thinking something was odd."

"When you went walking here, I bet you hadn't thrown away your dream of becoming a translator."

"Oh no—I was as determined to do something with my life as he was."

"If I were you, I'd go for it. Of course, it's too late for me now."

Denko stopped walking. Her head was drooping forward like a limp flower. Hugging Denko's body, Michiko sat her on a bench covered in peeling paint, white and brittle. Near the end lay a red Glico candy box. "That's right . . . That's certainly true." Michiko nodded in agreement as Denko transmitted her thoughts to her.

Back then, half playing and half in earnest, she'd told Yukio that one day, she would let him read a mystery she had translated. Actually, she had meant that. She had thought there was nothing impossible in this world. If you worked hard, you could get whatever you wanted. Dreams and pipe dreams became one, making every day sparkle with possibilities. But the succeeding years were busy in their various ways. The year their son entered grade school, Yukio gave in to the advances of a female doctor from his class and began having an affair. Michiko made plans to move out, going so far as to transfer their son to a different school. But Yukio soon parted ways with the female doctor, and life returned to normal. After that, he never entered into a relationship with another woman that his wife could find out about. Yukio himself said he had learned his lesson the first time. For these ten years, their son and his exams had come first.

"You're right . . . ," Michiko sighed. "I'm still alive."

"Yes, you are . . . I only got to live twenty-three years, but if you and the doctor add twenty-three years to your age, where does that put you?"

"Just over seventy, I suppose."

"You'll live at least that long, don't you think?"

"Probably, since neither of us has cancer in the family. Please, don't say any more. I already know what you want to tell me . . ."

Michiko stood up from the bench. The motion made the candy box fall to the ground. On the front of the box, a man was raising both hands in the air. Was he about to start running? Was he already running? She thought he seemed a bit young to be reaching his goal already. When Michiko crouched near the ground and peered closely at the box, she got the sensation that the man's legs were moving. She could feel Denko's breath behind her ears, but she thought she could make it now without looking back.

⁜

When the rain stopped, Yukio decided to practice putting in the yard. He opened the sliding door and stepped out, left foot first. As he began to slip into his outdoor sandals, he lost his balance and kicked a nearby object. His sandals and the dendrobium had been sitting on the same stone step. The flowerpot shot off the step to the ground below.

"Are you all right?" called Michiko, who was already out weeding.

"Fine," replied Yukio. When he tried to pick up the plant, the orchid popped completely out of the pot and tumbled onto the lawn, its roots wrapped around the dried potting moss. Michiko kept working without noticing.

Yukio picked up the orchid. Then, as if he were examining a patient, he looked closely at its naked body. Its stem had grown thick, round, and long, and it was still producing flowers. But the portion that connected to the roots was thin. Yukio was impressed that the plant had been taking in moisture through such a narrow passage. The plant looked off-balance, like a woman whose ankles are oddly thin for her size. The roots and the moss were dry enough for the plant to come out of the pot easily when tipped. Four flowers had just fallen off, but when Yukio put the plant back in the pot, it looked unchanged overall.

Returning the pot to its place, he put the four orphaned flowers in the palm of one hand.

"Michiko, about what we were discussing earlier—why don't you give it a try?" the husband said to his wife.

"Really? You'll agree to it? Thank you. I'd really like to see what I can do."

"No point in doing it halfway—keep at it till you see some results," Yukio added, subdued by his wife's pleased response. No matter how hard she studied, he doubted Michiko would ever gain the ability to make translation her profession. Then again, that hardly mattered. Once in summer and once in winter, she'd live in their son's apartment and take a special, one-month course, commuting to a vocational school with the young people. That much, Yukio wanted to let her do. The rest of the year, she would be home taking courses by correspondence, so there wouldn't be much of an effect on the household.

But still, Yukio thought, looking down at his wife's back.

Where was the wife who had been inexplicably withdrawn until a few days ago? Yukio had kept silent, worried that confronting her would only make things worse. Even if he told her a joke, she would merely move her mouth into the shape of a smile for two or three seconds, then slip back down to a deep place where he couldn't reach her. With dark, faraway eyes that betrayed no thoughts, she would stare through the TV screen, through the back of the cathode ray tube, through to the other side of the world. There were times when she was utterly unresponsive. Yukio could only keep his distance, sensing that the slightest remark could spawn a giant ripple effect.

Everything had taken a turn for the worse the day he brought the orchid home. He'd regretted it, wishing he had left it in the on-call room, but taking it back had seemed like more trouble than it was worth. He'd decided to leave it where it was. Then, in these past few days, his wife's mood had improved, and her color and energy had returned. Her spirit had grown youthful again overnight. When she transferred the orchid outdoors or indoors, she would hum to it under her breath, calling it Denko. When he asked why Denko, she said it came from dendrobium.

"Denko, of all names," Yukio said to the four flowers in his palm. "Sorry about that," he apologized. "I didn't come up with the name, my wife did . . ." Yukio's palm began to feel ticklish. Then his chest tightened with grief.

I will never forget the three and a half years I had with you . . .

A sudden flood of memories drove Yukio back into the living room, flowerpot and putter in hand. At the back of his neck he could feel the strength of her arms clinging to him, not letting go, saying she didn't want to die without once being held by a man. He still clearly recalled pretending to have a conference and taking her on an overnight trip: One year ago, seventh day of the New

Year, high noon, still asking whether he was enough for her, he had slipped his fingers into the opening in her soft pubic hair. His nails had been closely trimmed.

He also remembered the moment she had told him he should forget her and carry on with his life after she died. He had frozen in his tracks, wondering whether a nurse was listening at the door. The whole affair had begun with a feeling of sympathy; as a doctor he had done his best; above all, he had done everything in his power to fulfill the final wishes of a dying woman. All of these excuses he could make, but he sensed that the cause of his wife's depression lay with him, that he had a great debt to repay.

Yet how was it ending? With *Denko*.

Wry laughter rose in Yukio's throat. Maybe Denko wasn't such a bad name after all. "When you're reborn, come back as a sturdy woman who suits being called Denko," he murmured to someone who would never have fit that name.

First published, 1998
Translation by Avery Fischer Udagawa

Nobuko Takagi was born in 1946. She won the Akutagawa Prize in 1984 for her novel *Embracing the Light*. Takagi is perhaps best known for her explorations around the theme of love. Her fiction deals with love in many different guises: pure love, married love, extra-marital affairs, and love triangles. Her rich, sensuous prose often focuses on the dark side of human nature, and on the psychological mechanisms of love.

BIOGRAPHIES

FOREWORD

Ruth Ozeki is an award-winning filmmaker and novelist, whose work has been characterized by U.S.A. Today as "ardent and passionate . . . rare and provocative." Her novels, *My Year of Meats* (1998) and *All Over Creation* (2003), have garnered widespread glowing reviews and awards, and together they have been translated into eleven languages and published in fourteen countries. Her films include *Body of Correspondence* (1994), and *Halving the Bones* (1995), an autobiographical account of Ozeki's journey as she brings her grandmother's remains home from Japan.

Ozeki was born and raised in New Haven, Connecticut, by an American father and a Japanese mother. After studying English and Asian Studies at Smith College, she received a Japanese Ministry of Education Fellowship to do graduate work in classical Japanese literature at Nara University. During her years in Japan, she worked as a bar hostess, studied flower arrangement as well as Noh drama and mask carving, founded a language school, and taught in the English Department at Kyoto Sangyo University.

Ozeki is a frequent lecturer at universities and colleges throughout North America. She divides her time between New York City and British Columbia, where she is currently at work on a new novel.

JACKET ART

Tomoko Sawada was born in Kobe in 1977, and is one of the brightest up-and-coming stars of Japan's contemporary art scene. In her series of photographic self-portraits, she assumes a variety of physical identities, forcing the viewer to question the relationship between the inner woman and her outward appearance. To what extent are women consciously choosing to conform or differ in the costumes that they wear, and to what extent does society judge women by their looks? In the *ID-400* series (1998), from which an extract is reproduced on the cover of this book, Sawada takes 400 photo-booth shots of herself in a host of carefully crafted different guises. *Omiai* (2002) is a series of thirty photographs of Sawada in different formal outfits taken at a professional portrait studio. Japanese parents distribute these "omiai" photographs amongst their acquaintances in the hope of finding a suitable marriage partner for their children. *School Days* (2004) is a series of class photos of high-school girls in identical uniforms. Close inspection of the pictures reveal that all the girls are Sawada, and that in the midst of uniformity there are subtle variations in hairstyles, accessories, and facial expressions.

Sawada lives and works in Japan. She has won several awards, including the Kimura Ihei Memorial Photography Award in 2004, and has taken part in many solo and group shows in Japan, the United States and Europe.

TRANSLATION

Avery Fischer Udagawa grew up in Kansas and earned a B.A. in English and Asian Studies at St. Olaf College in Minnesota. She studied at Nanzan University in Nagoya on a Fulbright Fellowship, and at the Inter-University Center for Japanese Language Studies, Yokohama, with support from the College Women's Association of Japan. She is an editor, translator, and writer based in Muscat, Oman.

Louise Heal comes from Manchester, England. She holds a B.A. in French from the University of Nottingham and an M.A. in Advanced Japanese Studies from the University of Sheffield. She has a keen interest in contemporary Japanese literature, particularly by women writers, and has translated works by Taeko Kono and Setsuko Shinoda. She spent sixteen years in Japan where she taught English language and literature at high-school and university levels, and spent much of her spare time involved in community theater. She currently works out of Fort Worth, Texas as a freelance translator.

Hisako Ifshin left her native Japan for San Francisco in 1992 and has lived there ever since, working as a translator, writer, and journalist for Japanese and American print and digital media. In Tokyo she worked in advertising and journalism. She has academic degrees from Japanese and American universities in linguistics, journalism, and art history. Her previous literary translations include works by Seiko Ito, Kiyoko Murata, and Yayoi Kusama, and haiku by the poet Itaru Ina for the movie *From a Silk Cocoon*.

Cathy Layne comes from Liverpool, England, and has lived in Tokyo since 1996. She holds an M.A. in Advanced Japanese Studies from the University of Sheffield, and currently works as an editor, with a particular interest in contemporary literature and Japanese pop culture.

Leza Lowitz was born in San Francisco. She is a poet, fiction writer, critic, and editor, who has published a dozen books on Japan. A graduate of U.C. Berkeley and San Francisco State, she has also taught literature at Tokyo University. Among her awards are the Japan-U.S. Friendship Commission Award for the Translation of Japanese Literature from the Donald Keene Center at Columbia University (with Shogo Oketani), the PEN/Oakland Josephine Miles Award for Poetry, and a PEN Syndicated Fiction Award. She currently owns a yoga studio in Tokyo, where she helps young women value themselves so they don't end up like Miyuki in the story she co-translated.

Philip Price was born in Middlesbrough, England. He studied German and Russian at the University of Glasgow, and has spent extended periods of work and study in Austria and Russia. After graduation, he moved to Japan with the JET Programme to teach English in Shizuoka Prefecture. In 2002, he completed an M.A. in Advanced Japanese Studies with the University of Sheffield, focusing in his graduation thesis on the literature and society of the Korean minority in Japan. He lives in Tokyo, where he works as a translator.

（英文版）インサイド
Inside and other short fiction

2006年2月24日　第1刷発行

著　者　　大道珠貴、島本理生、室井佑月、内田春菊、藤野千夜、
　　　　　山田詠美、長谷川純子、高樹のぶ子

英　訳　　ルイーズ・ヒール、宇田川エイヴリ・フィッシャー、
　　　　　イフシン・寿子、リザ・ロウィッツ、キャシー・レイン、
　　　　　フィリップ・ブライス

発行者　　富田 充

発行所　　講談社インターナショナル株式会社
　　　　　〒112-8652 東京都文京区音羽 1-17-14
　　　　　電話　03-3944-6493（編集部）
　　　　　　　　03-3944-6492（マーケティング部・業務部）
　　　　　ホームページ　www.kodansha-intl.com

印刷・製本所　　大日本印刷株式会社

Printed in Japan
ISBN 4-7700-3006-1